TØ147030

Titles

Francis B. Nyamnjoh
Stories from Abakwa
Mind Searching
The Disillusioned African
The Convert
Souls Forgotten
Married But Available
Intimate Strangers

Dibussi Tande
No Turning Back. Poems of Freedom 1990-1993
Scribbles from the Den: Essays on Politics and Collective
Memory in Cameroon

Kangsen Feka Wakai
Fragmented Melodies

Ntemfac Ofege
Namondo. Child of the Water Spirits
Hot Water for the Famous Seven

Emmanuel Fru Doh
Not Yet Damascus
The Fire Within
Africa's Political Wastelands: The Bastardization of
Cameroon
Oriki'badan
Wading the Tide
Stereotyping Africa: Surprising Answers to Surprising
Questions

Thomas Jing
Tale of an African Woman

Peter Wuteh Vakunta
Grassfields Stories from Cameroon
Green Rape: Poetry for the Environment
Majunga Tok: Poems in Pidgin English
Cry, My Beloved Africa
No Love Lost
Straddling The Mungo: A Book of Poems in English &
French

Ba'bila Mutia
Coils of Mortal Flesh

Kehbuma Langmia
Titabet and the Takumbeng
An Evil Meal of Evil
The Earth Mother

Victor Elame Musinga
The Barn
The Tragedy of Mr. No Balance

Ngessimo Mathe Mutaka
Building Capacity: Using TEFL and African Languages as
Development-oriented Literacy Tools

Milton Krieger
Cameroon's Social Democratic Front: Its History and
Prospects as an Opposition Political Party, 1990-2011

Sammy Oke Akombi
The Raped Amulet
The Woman Who Ate Python
Beware the Drives: Book of Verse
The Wages of Corruption

Susan Nkwentie Nde
Precipice
Second Engagement

**Francis B. Nyamnjoh &
Richard Fonteh Akum**
The Cameroon GCE Crisis: A Test of Anglophone
Solidarity

Joyce Ashuntantang & Dibussi Tande
Their Champagne Party Will End! Poems in Honor of
Bate Besong

Emmanuel Achu
Disturbing the Peace

Rosemary Ekosso
The House of Falling Women

Peterkins Manyong
God the Politician

George Ngwane
The Power in the Writer: Collected Essays on Culture,
Democracy & Development in Africa

John Percival
The 1961 Cameroon Plebiscite: Choice or Betrayal

Albert Azeyeh
Réussite scolaire, faillite sociale : généalogie mentale de
la crise de l'Afrique noire francophone

Aloysius Ajab Amin & Jean-Luc Dubois
Croissance et développement au Cameroun :
d'une croissance équilibrée à un développement équitable

Carlson Anyangwe
Imperialistic Politics in Cameroun:
Resistance & the Inception of the Restoration of the
Statehood of Southern Cameroons
Betrayal of Too Trusting a People: The UN, the UK and
the Trust Territory of the Southen Cameroons

Bill F. Ndi
K'Cracy, Trees in the Storm and Other Poems
Map: Musings On Ars Poetica
Thomas Lurting: The Fighting Sailor Turn'd Peaceable /
Le marin combattant devenu paisible
Soleil et ombre

**Kathryn Toure, Therese Mungah
Shalo Tchombe & Thierry Karsenti**
ICT and Changing Mindsets in Education

Charles Alobwed'Epie
The Day God Blinked
The Bad Samaritan
The Lady with the Sting
Exhumed, Tried and Hanged

G. D. Nyamndi
Babi Yar Symphony
Whether losing, Whether winning
Tussles: Collected Plays
Dogs in the Sun

Samuel Ebelle Kingue
Si Dieu était tout un chacun de nous ?

Ignasio Malizani Jimu
Urban Appropriation and Transformation: bicycle, taxi
and handcart operators in Mzuzu, Malawi

Justice Nyo' Wakai
Under the Broken Scale of Justice: The Law and My
Times

John Eyong Mengot
A Pact of Ages

Ignasio Malizani Jimu
Urban Appropriation and Transformation: Bicycle Taxi
and Handcart Operators

Joyce B. Ashuntantang
Landscaping and Coloniality: The Dissemination of
Cameroon Anglophone Literature

Jude Fokwang
Mediating Legitimacy: Chieftaincy and Democratisation in
Two African Chiefdoms

Michael A. Yanou
Dispossession and Access to Land in South Africa:
an African Perspevctive

Tikum Mbah Azonga
Cup Man and Other Stories
The Wooden Bicycle and Other Stories

John Nkemngong Nkengasong
Letters to Marions (And the Coming Generations)
The Call of Blood

Amady Aly Dieng
Les étudiants africains et la littérature négro-africaine
d'expression française

Tah Asongwed
Born to Rule: Autobiography of a life President
Child of Earth

Frida Menkan Mbunda
Shadows From The Abyss

Bongasu Tanla Kishani
A Basket of Kola Nuts
Konglanjo (Spears of Love without Ill-fortune) and
Letters to Ethiopia with some Random Poems

Fo Angwafo III S.A.N of Mankon
Royalty and Politics: The Story of My Life

Basil Diki
The Lord of Anomy
Shrouded Blessings

Churchill Ewumbue-Monono
Youth and Nation-Building in Cameroon: A Study of
National Youth Day Messages and Leadership Discourse
(1949-2009)

Emmanuel N. Chia, Joseph C. Suh & Alexandre Ndeffo Tene
Perspectives on Translation and Interpretation in
Cameroon

Linus T. Asong
The Crown of Thorns
No Way to Die
A Legend of the Dead: Sequel of *The Crown of Thorns*
The Akroma File
Salvation Colony: Sequel to *No Way to Die*
Chopchair
Doctor Frederick Ngenito

Vivian Sihshu Yenika
Imitation Whiteman
Press Lake Varsity Girls: The Freshman Year

Beatrice Fri Bime
Someplace, Somewhere
Mystique: A Collection of Lake Myths

Shadrach A. Ambanasom
Son of the Native Soil
The Cameroonian Novel of English Expression:
An Introduction

Tangie Nsoh Fonchingong and Gemandze John Bobuin
Cameroon: The Stakes and Challenges of Governance and
Development

Tatah Mentan
Democratizing or Reconfiguring Predatory Autocracy?
Myths and Realities in Africa Today

Roselyne M. Jua & Bate Besong
To the Budding Creative Writer: A Handbook

Albert Mukong
Prisoner without a Crime: Disciplining Dissent in
Ahidjo's Cameroon

Mbuh Tennu Mbuh
In the Shadow of my Country

Bernard Nsokika Fonlon
Genuine Intellectuals: Academic and Social
Responsibilities of Universities in Africa

Lilian Lem Atanga
Gender, Discourse and Power in the Cameroonian
Parliament

Cornelius Mbifung Lambi & Emmanuel Neba Ndenecho
Ecology and Natural Resource Development
in the Western Highlands of Cameroon: Issues in Natural
Resource Managment

Gideon F. For-mukwai
Facing Adversity with Audacity

Peter W. Vakunta & Bill F. Ndi
Nul n'a le monopole du français : deux poètes du
Cameroon anglophone

Emmanuel Matateyou
Les murmures de l'harmattan

Ekpe Inyang
The Hill Barbers

JK Bannavti
Rock of God *(Kìlán ke Nyiíy)*

Godfrey B. Tangwa (Rotcod Gobata)
I Spit on their Graves: Testimony Relevant to the
Democratization Struggle in Cameroon

Henrietta Mambo Nyamnjoh
"We Get Nothing from Fishishing", Fishing for Boat
Opportunies amongst Senegalese Fisher Migrants

Bill F. Ndi, Dieurat Clervoyant & Peter W. Vakunta
Les douleurs de la plume noire : du Cameroun
anglophone à Haïti

Laurence Juma
Kileleshwa: A Tale of Love, Betrayal and Corruption in
Kenya

Nol Alembong
Forest Echoes (Poems)

Marie-Hélène Mottin-Sylla & Joëlle Palmieri
Excision : les jeunes changent l'Afrique par le TIC

Walter Gam Nkwi
Voicing the Voiceless: Contributions to Closing Gaps in
Cameroon History, 1958-2009

John Koyela Fokwang
A Dictionary of Popular Bali Names

Alain-Joseph Sissao
(Translated from the French by Nina Tanti)
Folktales from the Moose of Burkina Faso

Exhumed
Tried and Hanged

Charles Alobwed'Epie

Langaa Research & Publishing CIG
Mankon, Bamenda

Publisher:
Langaa RPCIG
Langaa Research & Publishing Common Initiative Group
P.O. Box 902 Mankon
Bamenda
North West Region
Cameroon
Langaagrp@gmail.com
www.langaa-rpcig.net

Distributed outside N. America by African Books
Collective
orders@africanbookscollective.com
www.africanbookscollective.com

Distributed in N. America by Michigan State
University Press
msupress@msu.edu
www.msupress.msu.edu

ISBN: 9956-616-53-2

DISCLAIMER

The names, characters, places and incidents in this book are either the product of the author's imagination or are used fictitiously. Accordingly, any resemblance to actual persons, living or dead, events, or locales is entirely one of incredible coincidence.

Contents

Chapter One 1

Chapter Two 5

Chapter Three 15

Chapter Four 23

Chapter Five 31

Chapter Six 37

Chapter Seven 63

Chapter Eight 71

Chapter Nine 83

Chapter Ten 89

Chapter Eleven 97

Chapter Twelve 105

Chapter Thirteen 129

Chapter Fourteen 137

Chapter One

The Witness

It was mid morning; the sun was unusually, but pleasantly hot for *Sango* Nkwel'Ngole. He asked his son Ebune to put out his wooden sofa for him to bask himself in the sun. In putting out the sofa, Ebune remarked that his father would feel better in hell than in heaven. He put it out and told him he had done so. *Sango* Nkwel'Ngole wobbled to the sofa and sat down. Presently, he felt the heat defrosting what he had considered ice in his veins. The bright sun hurt his eyes and so, he closed them to enjoy the benevolence of the sun more conveniently. Gradually he succumbed to sleep. Just when he started drifting into pleasant dreams, two boys came and woke him up.

"*A Sen* Nkwel'", they called and shook him. The old man started and opened his eyes rather abruptly. The rays of the sun pierced and hurt his eyes. In the blur of tears that oozed out of his eyes, he saw two figures.

"We have been sent to invite you tomorrow morning, very early, to the village grove," the children said. *Sango* Nkwel'Ngole blinked abnormally as he peered at the speakers to find out who they were. He did not recognize any of them. He asked who they were. They introduced themselves as Ntongwe and Mukala.

"Who has sent you," the old man asked.

"The people of Etambeng," they responded.

"Are there still people in Etambeng?" he asked.

"Yes. Those that dared the odds and came back," they answered.

"They are inviting me for what? How can I get to the grove? When I was Nkwel'Ngole people shunned my

1

presence in the grove. Now that I am no longer Nkwel'Ngole people are inviting me in the grove – what for?"

"There is a convention-shattering matter which we think only you can enlighten people on. You are the oldest and most knowledgeable person in this village now, the only living witness of things of old. We want you to come and tell us what happened that this village of Etambeng lost its population to other villages. That will enable people see whether we acted justly or not."

"My children, I would have willingly come to the grove to tell you what happened to Etambeng but unfortunately, I am weak-kneed and so unable to trek. Secondly, I wonder whether I can withstand prolonged and coherent recounting of events of old at this age. Look at me – a jacket of veins and bones, there is nothing here but veins and bones."

"*A sen* Nkwel', we shall carry you to the grove. We shall make a fire for you. We shall give you all the comfort you need. We shall give you all the protection."

"OK. You will better give me a hint of what you expect me to say in the grove. Give me some background information."

"Yes, *a sen* Nkwel', we have done something the village considers an abomination. The village wants us to explain why we did it. We have said we can only say why we did it if you came and told the village what happened – what led to our action. To cut a long story short, we exhumed the corpse of the late Saviour, tried it, found it guilty of crimes against humanity then hanged and burnt it."

"Who is the late Saviour? Is that a Bakossi name?"

"The man was first known as Epoge, then Ngii and later on, Saviour."

"One man, so many names? If my body does not disintegrate by tomorrow morning, I shall come with you. You have promised me maximum comfort and protection, am I right? Wherever I go there must be a fire made for me to bask myself."

"You are right. We know that," the children responded and returned to meet their friends.

Early the next morning the children went for *Sango* Nkwel'Ngole and had him comfortably seated by a glowing fire in the grove before the people of the village came.

The people were surprised to meet the seven boys and two girls waiting for them in the grove. The children's strategy of being first in the grove disorientated the people. They simply obeyed the children as they ushered them to where they wanted them to sit; thus altering the customary sitting in the grove. Customarily, the people sat according to their Houses or kin groups in which House-heads or delegated spokespersons spoke for the group. In mixing up the people the children neutralized concerted reasoning. When everybody was seated, Ngwane moved to the centre of the grove and addressed the people.

Ngwane

People of Etambeng, we are happy that you all have come early. I believe we shall start early and end early. I shall be grateful if this meeting goes on fast and ends well. Two days ago when Mukala came and told me that you wanted to see us, it took me some time to rally my friends together. You know we live in widely dispersed villages. We had to make everything possible to get together and travel here overnight. We came pretty early and decided to come here straight instead of disturbing you in your houses.

We have not come here to be tried. We have not come here to be scolded at. In other words, we have not come here as criminals. It may be some of you see us as rodent that could be bullied at. Don't make that mistake. Don't behave otherwise towards us. That wouldn't pay. It may instead annoy us and backfire with devastating consequences. We shall want all of us to discuss this matter in a cordial manner.

As you see, we are nine, representing the nine kin groups of this village. When we got in here, we discovered that you had cleared the grove and arranged nine seats which signified that you were also keeping to the original nine kin groups this village once boasted of. But if you look carefully, you will see that you have only cleared one tenth of the size of the original grove. Everybody is now seated and there is still much space. That shows that the population of this village has dwindled considerably. Where are the people?

This meeting will therefore start with telling you what made the elephant trample the crab to death and the brook ceased. That will be followed by what happened after the brook ceased. I believe you understand what I am saying. You know the story which says, an elephant was sleeping. Then a fly came singing in its ear, 'Who will give me a knife to cut somebody's head? Who will give me a knife to cut somebody's head?' The elephant panicked on hearing that the speaker was looking for a knife to cut somebody's head, and so stampeded. In the stamped it trampled the crab the god of water to death, and the brook in which all animals drank water ceased. Now, who was responsible for the mishap – the fly or the elephant? That is the puzzle we are going to tackle here and now.

Now, let me warn each and every one of us here, all mouths are meant to eat but not all mouths are meant to talk especially in a situation like this. What I mean by this is that, we shall not tolerate open speech or questions from people who cannot draw inferences from intricacies or twists in the stories my collaborators and I will tell.

But before we say anything, I shall ask *Sen* Etumbe to tell us how he came to discovering that the corpse of the late Saviour was exhumed. I shall not tolerate violent coughing. Anybody who has TB shall raise his/her hand and shall be given permission to go and cough far from here. No questions. *A sen* Etumbe come forth.

4

Chapter Two

Sango Etumbe

People of Etambeng, about four days ago, I was woken up
early in the morning by cries, "Wowo, what I'm I seeing like
this! Wowo, what I'm I seeing like this! Wowo, what I'm I
seeing like this! Wowo, what I'm I seeing like this! Wowo
what am I seeing like this!" The cries came around the late
Saviour's compound. So I sent my son Ebong to find out
which woman was crying and why she was crying. Ebong
returned to tell me that it was _Nyango_ Mesang, the late
Saviour's widow. He said she did not respond to questions.
She simply rolled on the ground and cried. So I took water,
washed my face and went there. When I got there, I met
three women dissuading her from crying. I held her by the
hand and raised her up. I asked her why she was crying.
Instead of telling me why she was crying, she led me to
where her late husband was buried two months back. She
fell short of reaching the grave. She simply pointed at it
and indicated that I could go and see for myself.

A numbing sensation ran through my body. I took courage
and went there. To my consternation I found the grave
completely ransacked. It was half filled with soil as if after
the loot, the looters had tried to refill it but were chased
away by somebody. I asked her what might have happened.
She shrugged her shoulders and said two days ago, she went
to Ndoh to condole with the family of her late uncle. And
while people were discussing the cause of his death, (it was
alleged he took oath over the corpse of his son's child that
if he were responsible for the child's death, he should die in

5

two weeks and in two weeks he died) she heard some children saying that wizards should be eliminated in all totality in this community. That is, there should be no trace of them having lived at all. They boasted that they had exhumed the corpse of the late chief of Etambeng (the saviour), tried it, found it guilty of the misuse of the power of witchcraft and hanged it. She said she did not take them seriously. She brushed their talk aside, considered them as being truculent and provocative and decided to return to her asylum home without responding.

But on her way home something kept drumming in her heart. She felt the urge to visit her late husband's grave. So, she set out that early morning and discovered to her horror that her late husband's grave had been despoiled and the corpse might have been taken away. As I have said, the grave is half filled with soil, not very recent soil. Judged from the trample and re-sprouting undergrowth, and the fact that the footprints have filled up significantly, there is every indication that the deed might have taken place a month or two ago. So, I beat the *Muankum* drum, the drum of the deity inviting the whole village in my compound. Thank God, the village harkened to my call promptly.

We all said it was an abomination. The case had all the ramifications of a violent death and would need an elaborate cleansing of the population when all is said and done about it. And so it was necessary for the sages of the land to put their heads together and find out the truth about the corpse of the late chief. I asked them to go to the grave and verify. I said the village had to know what had happened to the chief's corpse.

The whole village then filed behind me and I led the way to the grave in silence. *Nyango* Mesang and the women who had gathered around were asked to stay behind in my compound. A few meters to the grave I stopped the procession and picked one elderly person from each kin group and proceeded with them to the grave. The selected persons examined the place scrupulously, did some rituals then invited six young men to remove the soil from the grave. Their task was easy. The soil was loose, and very soon, they hit the bottom of the grave and invited an elderly person to examine the grave. *Sango* Ndime stepped forth and strained his eyes to see. He breathed in stertorously then said:

Sango Ndime
Brothers, we have challenged the gorilla to a wrestling match. Let each person come and see for himself. The chief's corpse is not in the grave. As *Mue* Etumbe has said, let nobody comment on this matter until *Muankum* decides what to do. Comments may disorientate us. We must just file past the grave for each of us to see for ourselves what has happened. *A Sango* Etumbe, to where do we take this matter now? Your compound is not ideal. A case like this is better handled in a sacred grove. Ever since we returned from exile, nobody has thought of clearing the grove of this village. Where shall we incarnate *Muankum* to handle this matter? The people of this village have carried a he-goat on their backs. Even those still on exile will bear the scent of the he-goat.

The Witness
Sango Ndime's remarks numbed the people of Etambeng. They stood motionless for some time before *Sango* Ekane broke the silence.

Sango Ekane
A Sango Ndim', sacred groves are made by people. Whatever we shall call a sacred grove shall be a sacred grove to handle this matter. We can't now go clearing the sacred grove that has been overgrown for several years. This is a very urgent

matter. If *Sango* Etumbe opens his house for us, let us call it a sacred grove and tackle this matter. All we need to do is to send the women and the uninitiated away when we want to incarnate *Muankum*.

The Witness
The people of Etambeng accepted the suggestion and asked *Sango* Etumbe to allow them use his premises. He accepted and called on the aggrieved widow to tell the people what happened. But before she took the floor *Sango* Ndime intercepted.

Sango Ndime
Brothers, *Nyango* Mesang will speak. But before she speaks, I shall like us to ask ourselves whether we doubt what has happened. Is there a person here who thinks that the chief's corpse has not been stolen? When we were going to the grave, I expected to see the corpse thrown away and the burial clothes and blankets looted. That is what grave-thieves do. They steal the clothes and blankets and rebury the corpse. If we all agree that in this case the corpse has been stolen then we can now give the floor to *Nyango* Mesang. *Nyango* Mesang, the floor is yours.

Nyango Mesang
People of Etambeng, I have little to tell you. You all have seen with your eyes and borne witness that my husband's corpse is not in the grave. I have sent word to my two other co-wives to come so that we confront the village. A man's wickedness and capability to harm people end when he dies. In the same vein, hatred for him and the desire to revenge on him end when he dies. That is why our people say, 'Corpses have no enemies'. But it seems corpses have enemies in Etambeng. Two days ago when I went to condole with my uncle's family, I was stunned with what some

children said. They said they had exhumed the corpse of the chief of Etambeng, chief Ngii, tried it, found it guilty of crimes against humanity and hanged it. Although I thought they were just bragging, something told me later to take them seriously and go and find out about my husband's grave. This morning when I got to the grave, I found it ransacked. I started crying and when *Sango* Etumbe came, I took him to the grave. He saw what had happened and drummed to invite you there.

Sango Ndime
Can you tell us the name of any of the children who said they had exhumed the body of your late husband? Do you know any? Can you recognize any?

Nyango Mesang
Yes. They are Atume, Ntongwe, Ngwene and Mukala. They are the ones I can remember very well. If I see the others, I shall recognize them.

Sango Ebate
That will help us identify the criminals. But of all those children only Mukala lives in this village, the others live outside the village. It may be difficult for us to lay hands on them. To take them unawares we should send for Mukala and interrogate him. We can then send emissaries to the villages in which the other children are and ask the chiefs to send them to us. If they prove intransigent, *Muankum* will bring them.

Mukala
I am here and if you want the other children I can go for them.

Sango Ndime

A mue Mukala, come forth then and tell us what prompted you to exhume the corpse of the chief (the Saviour). Our people say prompt acknowledgement of guilt mitigates not only the crime but also the punishment. You have not drawn the dagger as we thought you would. We are thankful for that. Come forth then and tell us your version of the matter.

Mukala

I'll better go and call the other boys and even girls who participated in exhuming Mr. Saviour. Each of us has a story to tell and I believe it would be good if you heard the stories on the same day. We should fix a date.

Ndobe

Hei! Stop that pomposity. Shut up your mouth. You want a way to escape. You will not shake where you are. Stupid.

Mukala

Who are you howling at, me? Who gave you that audacity? Woman of a thing, you look straight into my forehead? You are small. You are insignificant, smaller than an ant in my eyes. Do you think we are afraid? Mr. Man, we have crossed seven streams. We have scaled seven valleys and seven mountains. What we have meted on chief Ngii whom you called Saviour, we shall mete on any other person found guilty of crimes against humanity in this village. You should not squirt bad breath at me. Your father will be the next. He will vomit all the children he is accused of having bewitched. Wait then, you will see. *Abuu*. Shit.

Ndobe

You nincompoop, what killed your father will kill you. I tell you, the maggots that ate your father will eat you. Your entrails are infested with witchcraft. Shit.

Sango Echome
"Hei! Hei! *A mue* Ndobe wait, wait. Please, be calm. *A mue* Mukala, you have said you are not afraid. You have said you would go and bring your collaborators. Don't take offence at minor things. Anybody here sees that you are frank. If you were afraid you would not have attended this meeting. So, I plead with this assembly that you be given time to go and get your friends. But before you do so, tell us where the corpse is.

Mukala
If the corpse is still 'alive', that is, if it is still physically preserved you will see on the day we shall all listen to what we have to say.

The Witness
After that sharp exchange of words, *Sango* Ndime tried to rebuild confidence and see how best the village would prepare to handle the matter.

Sango Ndime
Brothers…eh, eh, eh, *A Sango* Etumbe', eh, eh, eh. I cannot say the pipe-cleaner is broken in our pipe. In other words, I cannot say we have gotten to a stalemate. We have got the root of the matter. *Mue* Mukala has owned up and he says we should give him time to go and call his friends. Let's give him two days. Let's fix our next meeting a day after Eseh Market day, two days from today. By that time we might have cleared the village grove. This case has to be handled in its appropriate environment. That is, a place where *Muankum* decides cases akin to violent deaths. So, I propose that we disperse and tomorrow, early in the morning we should all meet at the village grove. Only men who tap palm wine and women will be exempted. The palm wine tappers will bring the wine and the women will bring food. The women should prepare food with whatever they have.

No woman should say she has no meat. Those who have mushroom should prepare it with cocoyam foofoo and *nzab'nge*. Those who can fish should go and catch tadpoles now for the same purpose. And those who can do neither of the two things should prepare bitter-leaf. All we need is good food and good palm wine.

The Witness

The assembly then rose and the people of Etambeng dispersed. The next day, the people got to the grove early in the morning. They cleared it and arranged the sitting positions according to the nine kin groups. *Sango* Ndime tried to remember where each kin group sat before the exodus. He could remember with certainty only where five sat. The rest, he guessed. Since there was no other knowledgeable person, the people accepted what he did. He asked them to sit in their places and advised that on the day of hearing the case, the kin groups should exhibit discipline. He said in a sensitive case like the one before them, each kin group had a definite role to play. So, people should not mix up.

In the afternoon, the women and palm wine tappers brought the food and wine and after the workers had eaten and drunk, *Sango* Ndime made them rehearse the proceedings of the next day. He advised them to prepare incriminating questions and ask them without fear or favour. Just when the people were about to return, *Sango* Mesue suggested prompt action against the children.

Sango Mesue

A Sango Ndim', I am flabbergasted by what those children have done. It is unheard of that a human corpse, a chief's corpse for that matter is desecrated. To me, there should be no trial or listening to those brats. They have already owned up their crime. For what shall we be judging them again?

When they come here we should pounce on them and catch them, tie them and punished them. They should be punished heavily. They should bring back that corpse.

Sango Ndime

A mue Mesue, what is in the stomach does not smell until it is farted or spoken out. Our stomachs are full of venom but let us be careful with the way we handle this matter. If the children acted irrationally, we cannot afford to act in the same manner. So, when they come tomorrow, we should show no hostility towards them. We should allow their insolence lead them into whatever punishment we shall mete on them.

Sango Mesue

I see your point. We should not make them have any cause for likening themselves to snakes. We all know that snakes are killed before they are tried. We should give them every opportunity to express themselves. But when they are found guilty, the axe of justice should fall heavily on them.

Eseme

We are discussing as if we are sure they will come. They have fled. Mukala came to eavesdrop on us and after getting what he wanted, he told his friends to escape. Those empty threats of crossing seven streams were just a camouflage. My wife saw him late in the evening yesterday going to Ndoh on his way to Twambe. They are gone.

Ebang

A mue, I don't think so. The steam that comes out of those children's mouths and noses, the way they chest-pound themselves when they are discussing that matter and the constant meetings they hold, are sure proof that they are not afraid. I shall not be surprised if the reverse happens in this case, that is, instead of us judging them they judge us.

Sango Etumbe

"Brothers, yesterday, I advised that we should not make comments on this case. *Sango* Ndime has advised that we prepare questions. We shall sit according to kin groups. Each kin group will be expected to ask at least one question to give the case a collective and fairly handled outlook. So, let's return to our respective houses and give ourselves the time to prepare the questions.

The Witness

After *Sango* Etumbe's advice, the people returned to their homes. The next morning they were surprised to meet the seven boys and two girls with *Sango* Nkwel'Ngole waiting for them in the grove. The children had broken all conventions. They had carried *Sango* Nkwel'Ngole to the grove very early in the morning, made a fire to keep him warm and were now receiving the people as if they were the custodians of the grove. And that is how it happened that the children, whom everybody had thought would flee from the wrath of the community, outflanked the elders of Etambeng and took them hostage. When everybody was seated, Ngwane stepped forth and called on *Sango* Nkwel'Ngole to tell the Etambeng village how and why Etambeng lost its population to other villages especially, Etaku.

Chapter Three

Sango Nkwel'Ngole
My village people, if I have lived for 100 years, then I have seen 100 things. This village, this Etambeng, when I was a child, was a village in which there were no orphans. There was abundance and the strong were generous. There was solidarity. There was patriotism. This village, this Etambeng didn't hunt with weapons. It caught buffalos with bare hands. But as life is, what is up today is down the next day. The yesteryears wise men of Etambeng gave way to the dunces of the horrible days we are here to recount. Our people say, a wise man living with foolish people develops elongated lips from constant sighing. I shan't consider myself a wise man but I have developed elongated lips from incessant sighing at the foolishness of the people of Etambeng.

In the evening we see Etaku glowing with lights. We hear music emanating from there and of course we know that the people dance in praise of their wellbeing. It has always been like that. The people of Etaku had developed and are developing their village into a semi-cosmopolitan town. Their sons and daughters in the Diaspora have each built a corrugated iron roofed house and visit the village at least once a year. Etaku has long standing electricity, pipe borne water, bars, and a daily market. So, for a very long time people from other villages have converged and are converging there on Sundays and main market days to have fun. Naturally, the girls from other villages, especially a neighbouring village like Etambeng scrambled to get married there. And of course, its inhabitants have been arrogant,

15

and downright insolent. Our people say, he who befriends the pig should learn to tolerate shit and must not complain when he's made to eat shit. But our people, Etambeng people thought they could befriend the pig and not eat shit.

One late evening, in fact, the night had really advanced, I can't remember the exact day, I heard the village crier's gong. *Gongggg, gongggg, gongggg,* no message. *Gongggg, gongggg, gongggg,* no message. I stretched myself on my bed. The pain in my sore clubfoot had just abated for me to have a nap when the gong shattered the expected peace. *Gonggg, gongggg, gonggg,* "Men, women and children of Etambeng", the message came finally. "Everybody should assemble at the village grove tomorrow morning. People should come along with their stools and they must come early," the crier announced. I woke up my wife *Nye* Mengongu, and told her the message. I told her not to disturb me if by the grace of God my pains allowed me to sleep till morning. I said she should get up early and go and represent me in the grove. Although I said that, I was itchy to go and listen to what was amidst. The anxiety to attend the meeting coupled with the pains worsened my insomnia. Sleep came towards morning and I overslept.

I got to the grove by a shortcut behind my kin group's sitting position, in fact directly behind where my wife sat. Now behind her, I heard her telling one of her friends that she woke up early in the morning and prepared breakfast for me because she thought I would want to eat immediately I got up because excruciating pains did not allow me eat in the evening. She said after setting the table, she left the house stealthily and got to the grove. People were already seated. Only chief Mukete was standing, apparently surveying the grove to find out who was there and who wasn't. Immediately he saw her, he howled, "*A Nye* Mengongu, where is your husband?"

She said she left me sleeping. That whenever she discovers that my pains have subsided and I am having a nap she never disturbs me. She added that she knew I would come once I got up. She emphasized that I was in terrible pains these days.

That response did not please the chief. He retorted, "Yes, that is how he is. When he comes late in a meeting, he wants it to be started anew. When he does not attend a meeting, he wants it cancelled and another held. Your husband is terrible."

I believe that remark made my wife lose her bearings. She retorted with a high pitched and disrespectful tone saying that I did not do those things intentionally. That any other handicapped person would not have been attending meetings at all. That her husband was brave and she had never seen a person in such pains devote himself to the well-being of his village. When she turned and saw me, she exclaimed and said, "Aha! Don't drain your venom. That is him there".

My wife's firm and rather contemptuous reaction confused the chief for some time. He remained pensive for awhile then said, "OK, then we can start". He then told the people that he had called them that early morning because of what had been splitting his ears. He said that if the flood gate of a rat mole's burrow is broken through, the rat mole dashes out through the escape hatch. He added that what the village was about to hear that morning would make them know whether their safety valve had been broken open or not. And if it were broken open, what would the village do? He then invited Esape to tell the village what he had to say.

Esape got up sullen and pensive. He ran his hands down his face as he moved to the centre of the grove, cleared his throat and addressed the people:

Esape

People of Etambeng, let me tell you. If it were possible for a person to wrench his heart out of his chest, I would have done so yesterday. Yesterday, I went to Etaku to visit my sister whom I heard was sick. When I was about to return, her husband said I should take a bottle of beer in the People's Bar. I told him I came up with a friend with whom I would like to share the bottle of beer. To make sure he did not have to buy two bottles for us, I told him to give me the money and return to his house. When he gave me the money, I entered the People's Bar and sat down to wait for *Mue* Bine. I bought the beer and asked for two glasses.

"You want to share one bottle of beer with somebody?" the bargirl asked contemptuously.

I sulked from shame. "No, I am waiting for a friend. Add another bottle. I'll start drinking mine before he comes," I said rather confusedly with stabbing shame and anger because the shame induced buying of another bottle of beer meant that I had to use the money my wife had sent for me to buy maggi cubes and other condiments for her. My friend soon came and we started drinking. We were in no hurry. We both liked the music. Then soon, three children from our village stepped forth to dance. As they danced, three despicable Etaku boys came in and pushed our children to the corner saying the centre was reserved for the sons and daughters of Etaku. They asked our children whether there were bars at Etambeng. My temperature rose instantly. Sweat sprouted all over my body. I lost the taste of my beer and asked *Mue* Bine to return with me. We both abandoned our beer halfway and called the boys to return with us. They pouted and continued dancing at the corner where they were pushed. Since we had expressed overt anger at the insolent Etaku boys we had no alternative but to return.

Sango Nkwel'Ngole

While Esape was still talking Ngalame interrupted, *"A mue, A mue, mue ye*. Please, please, wait, wait, wait let me speak, let me speak, let me embellish your words, let me complement what you have said". Ngaleme seized the floor from Esape.

Ngalame

People of Etambeng, I would have died of a swollen stomach if *Mue* Esape did not bring up this affair of the intransigence, oddity and pomposity of the people of Etaku. About three months ago, I went to Etaku and a friend invited me to the People's Bar – the same bar. As we drank, Nzole, one of our Etambeng daughters married there invited me for a dance. While we danced, a shrill cry pieced our ears. Nzole remarked that it was Esung who was being beaten by her husband. "People are tired of separating their fights. Everyday beating, everyday beating. People are fed up," she said in a noncommittal tone from which I deciphered a cross-to-the-other-side attitude. In other words, Nzole had acquired the spiting of Etambeng people attitude from her Etaku people.

Naturally I responded by ending the dance and going to see what was happening with one of our daughters. When I got there, I saw an unbelievable situation. Young men, women and the elderly stood watching Ekane beat the hell out of his wife. Our people say, one cannot say he has killed a snake until he has cut its head. It seems as if that is what the Etaku people say when it comes to beating our daughters married to them. They seem to say, they have not beaten our daughters until they have stripped them naked and rendered them unconscious. I swear to God, I saw our daughter stripped naked in the presence of women, men and children. She sprawled helpless on the ground. I believe she was in a coma. No Etaku woman took the courage to

go and cover our nude daughter. I stormed back home and
told her father *Sango* Mesumbe-me-Mbene to go and get his
daughter. I said it was better for his daughter to remain
without a husband than for her to go through that hell. That
is *Sango* Mesumbe. Ask him if he has gone. Our people think
it is a wonderful privilege for their daughters to marry Etaku
boys.

Sango Nkwel'Ngole
Nkede cut in, *"A mue, mue, mue,* let me also say something
about this Etaku syndrome".

Nkede seized the floor from Ngalame as he had seized
from Esape.

Nkede
We the people of Etambeng are daft when it comes to
dealing with the people of Etaku. We are all naïve. We render
ourselves inferior when we meet with them. We genuflect
before them and address even their non-title holders *Sango*.
When there is an occasion in Etaku we all attend. But when
there is an occasion here, even a death ceremony that requires
reciprocity, they don't come. Our chief, chief Mukete has
disappointed us several times in dealing with the people of
Etaku. We once told him that if the Sub-Divisional Officer
visits this area and invites us to a meeting at Etaku, we
should not attend. We should tell him that we are an
independent village. A few days later when the Senior
Divisional Officer invited us to a meeting there, we, his
subjects refused to go but he went. The chief of Etaku
now behaves as if this village is an appendage of Etaku.
Whatever mutual agreement we make, he and his subjects
abrogate with impunity.

I remember in the last joint meeting we held with them,
we agreed that they would stop their women from throwing
kitchen refuse in gutters when it is raining because running

rain water carries the refuse right onto our doorsteps. Is our village littered with kitchen refuse now or not? We also agreed that they would stop using poison in killing fish upstream because the stream is the source of our drinking water. But because they have pipe-borne water they don't care. A few days ago, our women and children were surprised by the amount of dead fish they found floating where we fetch drinking water. They reported it to the chief. Here he is. Did he react? Has he said anything?

Sango **Nkwel'Ngole**
Doctor Ebule interrupted Nkede. "*A mue, amue, mue ye, mue ye*, o, o, ooo, wait, wait, wait let me say something,"

Nkede grumbled but surrendered the floor to him.

Doctor Ebule
You, people of Etambeng, what *mue* Nkede has said is a criminal case and we should not take it lightly. I was a dispensary attendant for 16 years and I know the implications of what he and other speakers have said. When people throw kitchen refuse in gutters, the refuse decays and when rain water washes the dirt downwards the water carries germs. We cannot see germs with our eyes because they are very small. We can only see them if we use a microscope. It is not the dirt that is dangerous; it is the germs that are dangerous. It is because the people of Etaku throw dirt in gutters that our people get contaminated. If you judge it from the number of epidemic outbreak, you will see that epidemic outbreaks are more frequent in this village than in Etaku. Secondly when people drink wholly or partially poisoned water, they are exposed to health hazards. Our people are stunted and frequently sick because of the unfavourable health conditions the Etaku people have imposed on them.

I should also point out that, our people are poor because they spend their money in enriching Etaku bar owners. Our children don't go to school because they spend all their time dancing in bars at Etaku. Our men and women are promiscuous because of drinking and dancing in Etaku bars. People who are promiscuous are usually sterile. Look at the present population of Etambeng and compare it with what *Sango* Nkwel'Ngole said about the ancient Etambeng – Etambeng of giants that caught buffalos with bare hands. We have lost the focus for village development because we enjoy development facilities at Etaku. Our people say, he who sleeps on a borrowed mat soon finds himself sleeping on the ground'. We have found ourselves on the ground and it is time for us to take action. That is what I have to say.

Chapter Four

Sango **Nkwel'Ngole**

After that presentation of grievances, the grove fell dead silent. The people of Etambeng scratched their heads trying to think out solutions to their predicaments. At last Ebue, a young man from the House of Mehum stood up, moved to the centre of the grove and intoned a song.

Ebue
Solo : *Yaya, yaya, yaya, yaya,*
A be sang be mbog,, mbwog nye neh,
Chorus: *Yaya,*
Solo : *A be nya be mbwog, mbwog nye neh*
Chorus: *Yaya*
  Solo : *Nze Nye nabe nye nabe bob nen*
  Chorus: *Yaya,*
  Solo : *Nze nye bebeb nye bebeb bob nen*
Chorus: *Yaya,*
Solo : *Heee, mbwog nye ne,*
Chorus: *Yaya*
(Solo : Fathers of the land that is your land
  Mothers of the land that is your land
    If you will develop it do so now.
Chorus: Yaya)

Sango **Nkwel'Ngole**

Ebue raised his hands and dropped them, and the assembly responded with a resounding, 'ya'. Then he addressed the people.

Ebue

People of Etambeng, our elders say, it is not how long rain beats a person but how deeply it soaks him that chills him. I believe the Etaku rain has beaten us not only for too long but has also soaked us deeply – very deeply. I think it has soaked us to the childbearing nub. And who on this earth would want to expose the fontanel of his child to head-cracking? I can't blame the Etaku people. We have enslaved ourselves to them. As they sing, so do we sing. As they walk, so do we walk. If they say we should jump, we don't question. We simply ask, how high? Today, we have realized our folly. We have at last discovered ourselves and we must act. We must build an identity for ourselves and dispose of the crutches of dependence on Etaku. We must examine ourselves and find out what is Etaku in us and discard with it right now. Let's purge ourselves of Etakuism.

Sango Nkwel'Ngole

While Ebue was still talking, Etug'Ebang cut in and seized the floor.

Etug'Ebang

People of Etambeng, the spleen our brothers have vomited here is not strange to any of us. We have in one way or another been subjected to the spite and contempt with which the people of Etaku treat us. I have cut short *Mue* Ebue's speech because my bowels are turning. I don't think even if we gave him the whole day, he would say more. He has said the essential and now, it is for us to take action. If the elderly people cannot take action as *Sango* Mesumbe could not take, the young must take action right now. I suggest that we ban our people from going to Etaku to have fun in bars. I add that we ban our daughters from marrying the boys of Etaku. On the question of the women of Etaku throwing dirt into gutters for it to be washed onto our doorsteps, and the habit of Etaku people endangering our lives by killing fish with poison upstream, we should take the two issues to the DO. If he fails to solve them, we go to the Senior Divisional Officer himself. There is a limit to which we can tolerate those fellows poking their fingers into our eyes. I am saying this without mincing words. People who think they can't live without going to Etaku should be banished from Etambeng.

Sango Nkwel'Ngole

It may be Etug'Ebang had more to say, but the standing ovation he received was overwhelming. He was carried shoulder high and for a very long time, men, women and children danced to hail him. I shook my head at what I thought was the usual buffoonery of the people of Etambeng and laughed. To me the people were taking an emotional decision they could not sustain and chief Mukete in his usual naivety was encouraging them. I raised my hand, stood up in anger, got my crutches, limped to the centre of the grove, and blasted them.

People of Etambeng, I am beleaguered by what has been said, and our reaction to it. It is horrible that we have endured such humiliation for long from the people of Etaku. I am scandalized that our daughters have been undergoing untold barbarism in the hands of people we all thought were worthy of emulation, people we considered as the civilized people of this area, people we hailed for developing their village into a semi-cosmopolitan township. I am even more astonished that we have not taken any action to save them and let the Etaku people know that development is not only in infrastructure and entertainment centres. Development is also in the characters of the citizens of a given area.

The standing ovation *Mue* Etug'Ebang has received from us shows that we have now accepted to react in one accord and save ourselves from the embarrassment and barbarism we have enumerated. That is OK as far as rhetoric- induced emotions and stupidity are concerned. My father used to tell me that the broth of stupidity was better licked with the index finger than drunk with a spoon. I believe each and every one of us present here who has hailed *Mue* Etug'Ebang's decision to ban our interaction with the people of Etaku has drunk the broth of stupidity with the cooking spoon. I say that because I see the possibility of the people of Etambeng eating their vomit within the nearest future.

What *mue* Etug'Ebang has suggested, and the people of Etambeng have confirmed with a standing ovation requires preparation – putting alternative structures in place. Have we done so? I am saying that in all sincerity. Have you ever seen me and my children at Etaku? Those of you who are addicted to going to Etaku should have alternative places for fun. Once you have, I shall go on with you in hailing *Mue* Etug'Ebang. Now listen to me. I do not condemn *Mue* Etug'Ebang's suggestion. I have not said he is stupid. No, I haven't. All I'm saying is that we are not yet prepared to sever ties with Etaku. *Mue* Etug'Ebang could be ready. I know he is a disciplined person but are all of you disciplined?

We cannot fight the people of Etaku from an emotional standpoint, from the effects of rhetoric. They have had decades of steady growth. Their children are more educated, more patriotic and richer than ours. But the world did not start yesterday. I believe with adequate planning and good management, we shall catch up with them. We can even overtake them because pomposity and haughtiness will work against their growth. It has even started working against their growth. Do you know what curse the nakedness of a woman inflicts on children who take pleasure in watching nudity? We should allow our people interact with the people of Etaku while we built up our resources for development. We should not be antagonistic to them. We should relate with them in order to learn from them and imitate them. We should lay down development plans and evaluate our progress yearly. It is only when we do that that we can say we are moving forward. Sentiments are not the best option in a situation like the one before us.

The Witness

After saying that, Sango Nkwel'Ngole limbed back to his seat and sat down. The place was quiet for a very long time. He thought he had made a point that would be accepted. But before he congratulated himself, chief Mukete got up and admonished him.

Chief Mukete

Aha! Didn't I say it? Before we started didn't I say that Nkwel'Ngole always dismantles what people have built? What is happening now? See, what everybody has acclaimed, he is condemning and that is how he is. In fact I believe his lameness has warped his brains. I wonder how he rules his House. I pray that we don't lose our bearings. We should dismiss him as husk.

Sango Nkwel'Ngole

The chief's insults meant nothing to me. I knew I was right and he was wrong and so I got up to return to my compound. As I limped out of the grove, some people booed at me. That meant nothing to me. I returned in high spirits in the confidence that my wife, *Nye* Mengopngu who had remained behind to listen to the deliberations would tell me all that was discussed in my absence.

In the evening she returned with a bumpy face grumbling and complaining about the way the chief treated me.

Nye Mengongu

A Sango, I don't know what is happening between you and the chief. I don't know what you have done to him to merit such indignant and shabby treatment. I cannot remember an occasion that has passed without the chief rebuking and shredding you into pieces. At first he used to do so behind your back but of recent he has resorted to more aggressive and frontal attacks. Although the attacks do not seem to hurt you, they hurt us – members of your family. I could not help confronting his wife after you left the grove. I told her that the chief was in the habit of insulting you and saying you destroy things people have built. In her response she defended him by saying that it is you to blame for every act of discord. She said you always take the chief for a fool, and that you are insolent and contemptuous toward him. She said respect was reciprocal.

Sango Nkwel'Ngole
Should I now consider him a genus? That fellow is as stupid as mudfish.

Nye Mengongu
Now you see, you have just confirmed what his wife said – always calling him a fool. That is not correct. Whether he is a fool or not, he is the chief. Furthermore you should know that you are cousins. I think you must work out a more cordial way of talking to him. He tends to be nervous when you are around. After you had gone *Sango* Bwemine of the House of Bwesse suggested that he should send for you because it was imperative for all the House-heads to be present in taking major decisions concerning our interaction with the people of Etaku. The chief refused sending for you perhaps because he feared you would be on his nerves again. So, after debating for a very short while they banned marriages and visits between the two villages.

One boy, I think he is called Ndue, asked whether the ban extended to condolence visits. The boy pointed out that most of the people of Etambeng had paternal and maternal uncles in Etaku. Suppose one died, would the concerned person of Etambeng not go? If the concerned person went and he was entertained in a bar, what would they call that – a violation of Etambeng ban?

That renewed the debate again and after chewing their tongues trying to fashion out an all enlacing statement; they said that what they were against was irresponsible going to Etaku to drink. Then *Sango* Ekem'bepie of the House of Ekeme suggested that the people of Etambeng should ask their sons and daughters of the Diaspora to come and build bars in Etambeng. He said it was imperative for the village to have a bar equipped with music.

Sango Atume Nguse of the House of Nyed then said there was a very rich man at Mbomzii, a descendant of the House of Nyed who could be contacted and if he accepted, the village would give him a plot and he would build the bar. A delegation was then asked to look for the man.

Chapter Five

Sango Nkwel'Ngole

Several days later, there were manifestations of joy in the village. When I asked what was happening, Ebune, my son told me that the man was brought and taken round the village for him to choose where he would build the bar. He chose Esam and promised to start work in two weeks. Then he asked to be taken to Etaku to see how bars there looked like in order to build one that would be the envy of the people of Etaku. He promised that his standards would be so high that the people of Etaku and neighbouring villages would have no choice but to come to Etambeng. After that he returned and in two weeks brought building materials and builders to start the work. The people of Etambeng were so excited and were so eager to start work that they compelled Chief Mukete to send for all the House-heads of Etambeng including me to discuss the modalities of work and other matters. Although the pain in my leg was piercing, I attended the meeting. I thought it was imperative for me to attend because there was a loophole in the deal which I was obliged to correct. Our people say it is the weapon fashioned by father gorilla that kills baby gorilla. When the people came chief Mukete addressed them.

Chief Mukete

People of Etambeng, our people say, he who makes a promise counts the days. We have counted the days and the day of the promise has come. That is why I have called you that we organize ourselves on how the work would be done.

Our man has chosen Esam – a place overgrown with spiky grass and bushes. Although he has brought workers, the village has to help them in order to realize the project on time. I open the floor for suggestions.

Sango Nkwel'Ngole

Immediately the chief declared the debate open, *Sango* Nnange-Mbwoge put up his hand and took the floor.

Sango Nnange-Mbwoge
of the House of Nang

Sango chief, I suggest that we ask the man to look for paid labour. We are giving him a plot for free and if we give him labour too for free he won't have value for the place.

Sango Ngwese Esape
of the House of Nkong

I believed *Sango* Nnange has misunderstood the chief. The chief has not said that we constitute a permanent work force for the man. He has said we help in this initial stage. We may work for two or three days and once the place is cleared we leave what remains to be done to the man and his people.

Sango Ngwen'Ebong
of the House of Mehum

I think we could help the man for a day or two. That wouldn't kill us. But the man should be told to prepare good food and good wine.

Sango Nkwel'Ngole

I felt anger smoulder in me when I heard a numb skull reduce an important issue to food. I sighed, stood up and started moving away.

    Sango Ntongwe stood up and held me, urging me to stay to the end.

I snapped at him and said the stupidity of the people of this village worked on my nerves. I asked what relationship we had with the man he and his chief wanted to install at Esam. I wondered whether the chief himself knew. I asked whether the chief himself could tell us where the man came from. I reminded them that Esam was a ritually sensitive place, a place where a whole kin group had vanished. There was no single surviving person of Esam anywhere in the world. Now, without recourse to tradition, the people of Etambeng and their chief want to establish a non-member of Esam ancestry on the graves of its people? I pointed out that since they and their chief had decided on what to do; I who objected could not stay on. That was why I was going away.

After expressing my anger I left the place. Later that evening, I sent my son to call *Sango* Nyame Ngole. When he came I asked him how they ended the meeting.

Sango Nyame Ngole

A Sango Nkwel'Ngol', the day you will die in this village, this village will cease to be. You are the only knowledgeable person in this village. You are not only knowledgeable, you are also very frank. Your revelations brought all of us to our senses. Even the chief confessed that you were right. We remembered that ever since the House of Esam got extinct, three other people had tried to settle in the place. The three died within a few days of moving in. Since our man says Esam is the most strategic place for commerce in Etambeng, we came to the conclusion that before we start work there, a series of rituals should be carried out. The ancestors of Esam should be appeased. So, we have asked the man to send for a large cow, a large goat and three cocks. We intend to hold an elaborate *ndie* of appeasement in the place and all the House-heads have agreed that you will lead the village in carrying out the event. The chief has convened another meeting for tomorrow evening. Please endeavour to attend.

Sango Nkwel'Ngole

The next day I attended the meeting. Chief Mukete reminded the people about the revelations I had made the day before. He said the revelations had made them think twice and they had come to the conclusion that they would carry out a series of rituals headed by me to appease the ancestors of Esam. The chief said the people of Esam were extinct. The land they once occupied could not be abandoned indefinitely. Someday, people would inhabit it. The concern of the village then was, to hasten the process by appeasing the ancestors and once they were sure they were appeased, they would install whoever wanted to inhabit the land. It was an obligation that they reinstated the tenth House of Etambeng.

On hearing what the chief said, I reeled in anger, stood up and told him why I came to the meeting.

A Sango Chief, I have attended this meeting to express my total objection to the installation of that man at Esam. His installation at Esam will bring upon the whole village the wrath of our ancestors. If we install that man at Esam, we shall be scraping old scars. Let's cast our minds back to the past. What did our foreparents say happened to the people of Esam? Now we want to install a descendant of the betrayer of the Esam kings group on the graves of the betrayed. I shall not be present.

Sango Esambe raised his hand and seized the floor to tell me what he knew about Esam.

Sango Esambe

I was told that when German soldiers were pursuing *Sango* Nnoko, the paramount chief of Ekutekang, he sought refuge in the compound of the original chief of Etambeng at Esam. The chief defended him for some time but surrendered him to them when the Germans kept pressing on. The Germans then took *Sango* Nnoko to Buea where they executed him for treason. All the chiefs of Bakossiland then cursed the chief of Esam and chose the grandfather of the present chief as chief of Etambeng. Epoge's grandfather, brother of the disposed chief, fearing retributions at Etambeng, migrated from Nyed, settled at Ngab where he begot Nkome the father of Epoge and other children. I remember when I was young his father always came here to participate in marriage and death celebrations of the House of Nyed. Epoge is one of us, a very highly educated person we should be proud of. He, unlike other highly educated persons decided to do business instead of working with government. So we should not doubt his ancestry.

Sango Nkwel'Ngole
Sango Esambe's intervention flared me up the more and I told him my mind.

A Sango Esambe, you see, it is not the identity of Epoge that will make me succumb to your desire to have him violate the sacredness of Esam. I have told your chief that I am opposed to Epoge's installation at Esam. I can only protest by word of mouth but let me warn you that those of you who will violate my advice will reap the consequences three folds. Now, let me be very clear with you. I shall not participate in anything that deals with the installation of Epoge at Esam. You and your chief can go ahead.

I am returning to my house. The fate of this village is in your hands.

With that, I returned to my house with a throbbing head. In the evening, *Sango* Nyame Ngole visited me and told me how the meeting went on in my absence.

Chapter Six

Sango Nyame Ngole

A Sango Nkwel'Ngol' I have always said that the day you
will die in this village, the village will cease to be. After you
left, the chief said he will never invite you for a meeting
again. He said you were arrogant and you always thought
you were the only intelligent person in Etambeng. He said
he thought your cancerous clubfoot has affected your brains.
Sango Bwemine said the village should ignore you and go
ahead with the work. He added that you were contradicting
yourself. When people suggested that we ban going to have
fun at Etaku, you advised that we should put alternative
structures in place before implementing the ban. Now we
were struggling to put the structures in place and you are
opposing. So he doubted where you stood.

All House-heads then agreed to go on with the work.
But as people were about to rise, *Sango* Ngwes'Esape
cautioned them. He said he now understood why you were
insisting that Epoge should not be allowed to build at Esam.
He said he remembered that ever since the House of Esam
got extinct, all the people who had tried to settle there had
died within the first week. So, there should be something
wrong with Esam which the village has failed to investigate.
People talk of a murderous totemic python inhabiting the
place. The power of a totemic animal ends when those who
owned it die. Why should the totemic python of Esam be
more powerful after the people had all died out? The
assembly sat silent for a long time. Finally, *Sango* Ekem'bepie
stood up and said that if there was any force that destroyed

people at Esam, it could not be anything, but a kin group force – the force of the House of Esam. A kin group force could not be above the collective forces of the Houses that constitute Etambeng. He therefore suggested that we assemble the forces of our individual Houses and use them to re-enforce Epoge so that when we install him at Esam he wouldn't lose a lock of hair.

Sango Ekem'bepie received a standing ovation for the suggestion and the House-heads of Etambeng unanimously agreed that they would re-enforce Epoge with all the forces at their disposal. So next Tuesday, after the Mkak market, the House-heads and their subjects will re-enforce Epoge with their respective powers.

Sango Nkwel'Ngole

What *Sango* Nyame Ngole told me made me develop palpitation.

"*A mue*," I called him. "I am devastated. Was the chief there?"

"Yes, he was."

"What did he say?"

"He simply applauded."

"He applauded? Is he in his right senses?"

We sat silent for a long time. At last, I sighed, brought out a kola nut broke it and we ate and drank the bottle of palm wine Ebune had kept for me. *Sango* Nyame then returned to his house while I nursed the sorrow in me. On Monday evening the village crier summoned all Etambeng people to the grove to re-enforce Epoge and thus make him immune to the evil forces of Esam. Nobody invited me, and so, I did not go but my wife, Nye Mengongu went. When she returned she told me what happened.

Nye Mengongu

A Sango Nkwel'Ngol', I believe you are stuck in the throats of the Etambeng people like a fish bone. Whenever they snub you, one person comes up to uphold your stand. The chief started the meeting by making a roll-call. He called every House-head by name but skipped yours. When he ascertained that all were there, he reminded them why they were there. He said they had assembled in order to bestow their ancestral powers on Epoge so as to make him a citizen of Etambeng and to immunize him against the evil forces of Esam. He then asked each House-head to produce the talismans of their kin group groves. Seven kin groups stepped forth and produced an array of ancient pots, gourds, horns and other containers of their ancestral powers.

Sango Ngwese Esape was asked to lead in rehearsing the general purpose incantation for the occasion. He fumbled twice trying to remember the exact words. Everybody was surprised that a House-head could not recite the general purpose incantation. In anger *Sango* Nyame Ngole asked where you were. The chief responded that you had refused to come. "Then we better postpone the occasion," *Sango* Nyame said rather angrily. "Talismans work in collaboration with incantations. In fact talismans derive their power from incantations. And everyday they are revitalized with incantations. Any guess or wrong rendition of an incantation renders the talisman ineffective and even dangerous – dangerous in the sense that the bearer of the talisman could venture into dangerous places thinking he had protection. That is why our forefathers trained individuals with sharp memories to memorize incantations. The only knowledgeable person among us now is *Sango* Nkwel'Ngole. If he is not here we should send for him. We should send for him. There is no way out."

"Did any emissaries come here?" my wife asked.

"Yes, they came. They said that the chief wanted to see me in the grove to help them recollect the collective incantation to prepare for the installation of Epoge at Esam. I asked them whether the chief was in his right senses. I told them that the collective incantation was the prerogative of the chief or a person designated by him. The collective incantation was the verbal insignia of authority. And so, it could not be used abusively. After saying that, I refused to follow them to the grove. They pleaded for a long time but I stood my grounds and they returned to the grove without me."

I might have been absent minded or it may be they returned when I had gone to ease myself. I did not take note. No doubt we waited for a long time before things started again. *Sango* Bwemine was then asked to lead the rehearsing exercise. He too fumbled and it was agreed that a second powerful delegation should be sent to you.

"Yes the delegation too came but I refused to follow them to the grove."

When the second delegation returned without you, the chief snapped, "I have told you that Nkwel'Ngole does not wish this village well. I have told you that his sore foot has affected his brains. You insist that we send for him. Where is he now? Let's go on with the preparations and by tomorrow some of us should be able to recall the words."

After a few more babbling, the people dispersed with the hope that by the next morning some of them would be able to recall the words of the incantation.

Sango Nkwel'Ngole

By the time Nye Mengongu concluded the narration, I was drenched with sweat. I admired her ability to recount events. But then, I thought she missed out in some important issues. So I sent for *Sango* Nyame Ngole. This is what he told me.

Sango Nyame Ngole

A Sango Nkwel'Ngol', our people say, if you acknowledge the superiority of your elder brother, carry his stool. I don't know why Etambeng does not want to carry your stool. You are adamant on this issue. Nobody wants to find out why you are opposed to the installation of Epoge at Esam. They simply blame you for being arrogant.

Seven House-heads presented their kin group powers to the chief. I refused to present mine until I saw you present yours. The chief might have been too preoccupied with other matters or with your refusal to come to the grove that he did not take note that I had refused to give the powers of my kin group until I saw you do so. The investiture of Etambeng sacred powers on Epoge will take place very soon. There is debate on who would lead the occasion. As of now, there is nobody capable of reciting the collective incantation. So, there are possibilities of either postponing the occasion or coming to plead with you to change your mind. So long as I am concerned, if you don't lead, I shall not participate.

Sango Nkwel'Ngole

After listening to *Sango* Nyame Ngole, I reproached himself for underrating my wife's report. She had made a more comprehensive report. However, I was happy with the revelations *Sango* Nyame Ngole made especially his support for me. I pondered over a thousand ways of foiling the occasion. Only one was feasible. If the rendition of the collective incantation were left into my hands, I would adulterate it and render the talismans impotent. Unfortunately, on the day of investiture, though I had expected the chief to send for me, he did not. So I sent my son Ebune, and my wife Nye Mengongu, to represent me. In the evening they returned and made these reports.

Nyeh Mengongu

A Sango, the whole occasion went on without even a fly mentioning your name. It seems as if the chief got somebody from another village to do the incantation. The person was very good. Everybody praised him. People said they had never heard such a mastery of the art. It was wonderful. When the women ululated they said:

If the lame won't recite incantations,
If the lame won't recite incantations,
If the lame won't recite incantations,
If the lame won't recite incantations,
Nephews will recite, O.
A belobo nso,o,o
O, nso, nso, O, nso, nso O.

Although I knew they were referring to you, I kept quiet. *Nyango* Mesang, the chief's young wife was very provocative.

Ebune

Papa, the chief sent for his maternal cousin *Seh* Metug'Mebwe from Etaku, who grew up here in Etambeng. He is the one who performed the collective incantation. Because he grew up in this village, he knew the names of all the ancestors. He was so fluent in rendering the incantation that everybody thought you would not have done better. It was wonderful. I am a young man but I can distinguish between well enacted and badly enacted incantation. *Seh* Metug'Mebwe's voice laced with enchanted mystical overtones echoed in the hills and mesmerized the living and the dead. At times, he blended the rhythm of incantation with that of the songs sung in invoking *Muankum*. The overall effect was overwhelming. One could tell the spellbinding effect on the population. As he performed, I saw an ecstatic *Seh* Nyame Ngole raise his staff of peace in unison with the other House-heads and feign a victory dance.

After the collective incantation, Chief Mukete made ten circles with wood ash in front of each House-head, and asked each of them to place his container of talismans by his circle. There was no person at the tenth circle – the circle adjacent to his. There, he placed a stool reminiscent to his. He invited Epoge and asked him to take off his shirt. Epoge took off the shirt and threw it on the ground. Then the chief asked him to stand by *Sango* Atume Nguse's circle. Epoge stepped forth and stood as he was asked to. Then the chief told *Sango* Akume Nguse to invest his powers upon Epoge.

Sango Atume Nguse, House-head of the House of Nyed thus led in the investiture of powers. He was dressed in traditional regalia – red cap with a loose hanging dome adorned with cowries, a necklace of the fangs of lions, a white shirt that was made to fly over his black loin cloth, a staff of peace in his left hand, and a broom of peace in his right hand.

He asked Epoge to stretch his hands. Epoge stretched his hands. *Sango* Atume Nguse incised Epoge's wrists, forehead and ankles. Then he took out of his *nguem* a small bottle containing black powder. He poured the powder in his left hand, spat into the powder and stirred it with his index finger. Then he rubbed the paste vigorously into the incisions saying, "On behalf of the chief, House-heads and people of Etambeng, I, Atume Nguse, (the whirlpool of the House of Nyed, the crest of Kupe Mountain, incarnator of Muankum) immunize you against all spiritual and physical attacks at Esam. Let this inoculation penetrate your system and be a protective shield against all weapons of witchcraft fashioned against you and your family. Be as hard as granite. Let no human being be capable of breaking you.

Ebune

Sango Atume Nguse searched into his *nguem* again, got *alligator* pepper, chewed it and spewed it onto Epoge's temple, chest and back and asked him what name he would like to be called after the investiture of powers. Epoge chose the name **Ngii**. *Sango* Atume Nguse then took the necklace of the fangs of lions from his neck and put it on the neck of Epoge saying,

Sango Atume Nguse

The name you have chosen ties in with what I expect from you. Wear this necklace of the fangs of lions and from today, you shall not only be Ngii by name but by word and deed. *A* Ngii I imbue you with the powers of my House so that you can be the lion you have chosen to be. Devour your enemies, great son of Etambeng. Crush their bones for the whole world to hear, and when they hear they should behold you with awe. Wherever you go, instil fear in the people. Be powerful. Be great.

Ebune

After that, *Sango* Atume Nguse told Epoge to step into *Sango* Ekem'bepie's circle. *Sango* Ekem'bepie stood up and placing his two hands on Epog's shoulders said,

Sango Ekem'bepie

A Ngii, from your looks and courage, you are a real ngii. But you are first a human being before being a fierce animal. We denuded you to see whether your flanks were saggy and needed re-enforcement. We have seen that they are satisfactorily full. You are as full as a jog of early morning palm wine. You are a man. As a man, you have climbed the iroko tree of *Ahon* Society. You have caught *Muankum* by the tail. You have caught the buffalo with bare hands. Receive the powers of my kin group and by this traditional

regalia I put on you, be a man amongst men so that whatever
meeting you attend, you should be listened to and not spoken
to. Be the spokesperson of both Etaku and Etambeng.
Subjugate the people of Etaku.

Ebune
Saying that, *Sango* Ekem'bepie clad Epoge with a
multicoloured traditional regalia – a regalia that bore the
insignias and colours of all cults in Etambeng. *Sango*
Ekem'bepie then asked Ngii to step into *Sango*
Ngwene'bong's circle. *Sango* Ngwene'bong rubbed his hands
together and said,

Sango Ngwene'bong
A Ngii, advice is like a walking stick. The strength of a
walking stick lies in the strength of its beholder. The strength
of advice lies on the strength of the advised. I don't doubt
your prowess. I am simply complementing what you are
already. Receive the powers of my House. Let nobody on
earth be capable of overcoming you. Be ngii as you have
requested.

Ebune
Sango Ngwene'bong gripped ngii in a mock wrestling match
and shook him, testing the strength of his muscles. Ngii
stiffened his muscles to the satisfaction of *Sango*
Ngwene'bong. He shook his head approvingly. Then he
asked Ngii to move into *Sango* Nnange'Mbwoge's circle. *Sango*
Nnange'Mbwoge coughed twice to clear his throat, then
addressed Ngii,

Sango Nnange'Mbwoge
A Ngii, receive the powers of my kin group and be the
buma tree of Etambeng so that wherever and whenever
you meet with the people of Etaku you should subdue them

as you will subdue the evil forces of Esam. Let no night weapon fashioned against you and your family, penetrate your defences. Be like the door of Etambeng, see the inside and the outside.

Ebune

Sango Nnange'Mbwoge massaged Ngii's hands and feet, placed his hands on his forehead and ran the hands down from his face down to his toes and hit the ground with both hands. He then stepped aside and gave the floor to *Sango* Bwemine. *Sango* Bwemine looked perplexed and as if from sleep said,

Sango **Bwemine**

A Ngii, I have little to say. I don't doubt your courage. Be as resistant as the spiky grass which when it is cut today, the next day, it sprouts again. I whole heartedly give you the powers of my House.

Ebune

Sango Bwemine gave the floor to Sango Ngwese Esape.

Sango **Ngwese Esape**

A Ngii, everything you have been given here fits you. You are clad in the apparels of *nhon, epie, mal,* and other cults of this great village. Not one single patriarch has hidden anything. I add the blessings of my House. Shine amongst us. Remove us from shame. Protect us. In order to do all that, receive the powers of my House, the House of Nkong where the springs of fertility flow for young girls to drink and become fertile and fill the village with children. Whosoever says what is good should not come your way, should be stricken by thunder.

Ebune

Sango Ngwese Esape then gave way to *Sango* Nyame Ngole.

Sango **Nyame Ngole**

A Ngii I come forth to confer onto you the powers of the House of Muanyam. I am not as full of joy as other brothers are because you would have now stepped into the circle of *Sango* Nkwel'Ngole. He is absent and I feel the vacuum. I believe something would be lacking if we carry out this investiture without him. You will be carrying half a jog of the investiture. He who carries a half-full jog of water or palm wine wobbles in movement. I would have liked that you carry a full jog of this investiture so that you walk steadily. And if you walk steadily, then we shall walk steadily. So, I still plead that the chief should send for *Sango* Nkwel'Ngole to complement what the other Houses have done. While waiting for that to happen, I confer onto you, without reservation, the full powers of the House of Muanyam. Be powerful. Subdue anyone who challenges you. Devour those who wish you harm. Neutralize the forces of Esam. Build there and fill the place of the tenth House of Etambeng. Let the nations have stories to tell about you.

Ebune

After saying that, *Sango* Nyame Ngole moved to his seat expecting the chief to send for you. The assembly remained silent for a long time before the chief reacted. He chose two House-heads to discuss the matter with him in a closed committee and after they had conferred, he announced that sending for you would slow down the ceremony. The chief said you would be made to confer your powers on Ngii in another occasion. So, they skipped your circle and Ngii stepped into the chief's circle. The chief took his time before he addressed the people.

Chief Mukete

People of Etambeng, today we are witnessing the reinstitution of the tenth kin group of Etambeng. Although *Sango* Nkwel'Ngole is not here, we count him as one of us unless he has decided to pull out of the Houses that constitute Etambeng. We are investing our powers on Epoge who has chosen the name Ngii. We believe that the evil forces that caused the extinction of the House of Esam, would have no powers over him. So far, the ceremony has gone on very well. Those who thought it would fail because of the absence of their expertise should be ashamed of themselves. I am the chief of this village. As I own you, so do you own me. I would have suggested that we rule out Nkwel'Ngole completely from this renovating phase of Etambeng. But my advisers say we should give him the chance of investing the powers of the House of Meliog on Epoge at a later date. I accept. I accept reluctantly because our people say, a single hand does not tie a bundle.

House-heads, in the presence and approval of the members of their Houses have conferred on Ngii defensive shields – shields to protect him against spiritual attacks at Esam. I wholeheartedly complement what they have done with the shields of my House. But let us not forget that he who bears only defensive shields can never win a war. He must possess offensive weapons for counterattack. We are now going to confer on Ngii powerful counterattack weapons so that if the forces that eliminate people at Esam are remote controlled by a person or persons in this village or elsewhere, he can fight back with devastating effects. Ngii is going to make a second round to receive the powers of offensive weapons. Let's start with *Sango* Atume Nguse again.

A Mue Atume Nguse, of the House of Nyed, what is in that pot?

Sango Atume Nguse

The pot contains the potions that cause yaws, leprosy, chickenpox and smallpox. They can be applied independently or collectively for greater effect.

A Ngii take the potions. If you concoct them and fire the mixture at your enemy they will inflict the diseases mentioned.

Chief Mukete

A Ngii step into the next circle, that of *Sango* Ekem'bepie.

A Sango Ekem'bepie of the House of Ekeme what is in that container?

Sango Ekem'bepie

The container contains *ngokume* that swallows children and livestock. *A* Ngii I offer it to you. Take it and when you bewitch a person swallow him as a python does its prey. Let there be no witchdoctor that would redeem a person you bewitch.

Chief Mukete

A Ngii step into the next circle, that of *Sango* Ngwene'bong.

A Sango Ngwene'bong, (House-head of the House of Mehum) what is in that pot?

Sango Ngwene'bong

The pot contains the potion that causes heat in the body, body pains, general disorders, headache and nose bleeding.

On behalf of my House, I offer it to Ngii. *A* Ngii, take it and when you fire it at your enemy he and his household will be stricken with the diseases mentioned.

Chief Mukete

A Ngii step into the next circle, that of *Sango* Nnange Mbwoge.

A Sango Nnange Mbwoge (House-head of the House of Nnang) what is in that horn?

Sango Nnange Mbwoge
The horn contains the whiskers of tigers. They cause tuberculosis. On behalf of my House, I offer it to Ngii. *A Ngii*, take them and when you fire them at your enemy, he should be afflicted with tuberculosis.

Chief Mukete
A Ngii step into the next circle, that of *Sango* Bwemine.

Sango Bwemine (House-head of the House of Bwese) what is in that bottle?

Sango Bwemine
The bottle contains the sperm of infertility. It renders women barren. If you have spiritual intercourse with a woman, you render her infertile. I wholeheartedly offer it to Ngii. *A* Ngii take it and use it when need be.

When you want to destroy a family, sleep with the women in their dreams and render them infertile, not only the women but also the livestock.

Chief Mukete
A Ngii step into the next circle, that of *Sango* Ngwese Esape.

A Sango Ngwese Esape, (House-head of the House of Nkong) what is in that clay pot?

Sango Ngwese Mesape
The pot contains the potion that causes blindness. Here it is. I offer it to Ngii to render blind all those who oppose him. Let him take it and apply it as he wishes.

Chief Mukete
A Ngii step into the next circle, that of *Sango* Nyame Ngole.

Sango Nyame Ngole (House-head of the House of Muanyam) what is in that tin?

Sango Nyame Ngole

The tin contains the potion that causes madness. I offer it to Ngii as the village of Etambeng as demanded. Let Ngii, take it and when he fires it at his enemy he shall go mad.

Ebune

After *Sango* Nyame Ngole's circle, the next one was yours. Since you were not there, chief Mukete asked Ngii to jump it and step into his circle. He eyed Ngii admirably and addressed him.

Chief Mukete

I am the embodiment of all that you have been given. Now, by all the traditional powers I inherited from my father, who also inherited from his father, who also inherited from his father's, father's father to the founder of Etambeng, I confer this *ngalemudumbu* onto you. When you load it with the items here given to you, it will never miss. It is the night gun, the mystical gun our fore-parents used to fight, conquer and drive away neighbouring tribes from this fertile land. It is both a defensive and an offensive weapon. Take it and use it for self-defence. But if you are provoked, use it for offensive purposes.

Make a last round, this time on your own. Nobody will escort you this time. Power is never given. It is seized. When you get to a House-head, take a bit of his sacred power from his container and put in yours. After taking from all containers, go and sit down on the tenth stool of the village of Etambeng.

Ebune

Ngii got a large empty container and moved from one House-head to another, scooping out sacred powers from their containers into his. In each case, he scooped out more than three quarters of the content of a container and put it in his. When he finally got to that of the chief and scooped, taking almost all of it, the chief joked, "You have left nothing for me?", and burst into a guffaw. The rest of the people mistook the guffaw for a compliment and gave Ngii a standing ovation.

The chief then put a traditional cap with a loosely hanging dome adorned with cowries on Ngii's head. Then he asked three House-heads to spread the skin of a lion in front of Ngii's stool, the last stool, and make him sit on the stool and rest his feet on the lion skin. After that, the chief led the way in shaking hands, bowing and expressing appreciation. When it came to the turn of the women, they genuflected, sealed their mouths with cupped hands in adoration, and filed past, ululating and making weird shrieks. It was now getting too late, so the chief postponed the other manifestations to next day. Tomorrow we shall go to complete the investiture of powers on Epoge.

Sango **Nkwel'Ngole**
Ebun', are you sure you are telling me the truth? I hope you are not making up stories.

Ebune
What do I gain in telling you lies. I am telling you what happened and how it happened.

Sango **Nkwel'Ngole**
Where did they keep the containers of the talismans?

Ebune
They left them on the same spot.

Sango **Nkwel'Ngole**
In the grove?

Ebune

Yes, in the grove. But Ngii promised to keep guards there. Tomorrow, each House-head will carry his container, and in a procession, the whole village will move from House to House to return the containers in their respective shrines.

Sango Nkwel'Ngole

To return the virtually empty containers in their respective shrines! Furthermore, do those fools know what will befall what is left in their containers this night? Oh!

Ebune

I am also very sceptical with the way things are happening.

Sango Nkwel'Ngole

Wowo! I can't believe that out of the eight House-heads who participated in the investiture of powers none could reason and caution his friends against that suicide. I would have sent you to Kata village tomorrow but since you say they will continue tomorrow, I shall want you to go and represent me.

The Witness

The next day, Ebune went to the grove early to make sure he missed nothing. He followed the developments scrupulously. In the evening he told his father, *Sango* Nkwel'Ngole what happened.

Ebune

When all were assembled, the chief asked each House-head to carry his container and follow *Sango* Atume Nguse in a procession. When the procession got to *Sango* Atume Nguse's House, he and the chief entered the shrine and put the container in its place. When they emerged from the shrine, the women ululated and shrieked and danced. *Sango* Atume

Nguse offered Ngii a cow and made him an honorary member of his House. From *Sango* Atume Nguse, to *Sango* Ekem'bepie, to *Sango* Ngwene'bong, *to Sango* Nnange Mbwoge – they followed the order they had used the previous day in the investiture of powers. Each House-head offered Ngii a valuable gift.

Ngii was in his traditional attire. Those who beheld him in his multicoloured dress, necklace of the fangs of lions, cap with a loosely hanging dome and staff of peace, were amazed. They could not remember whether they had seen a cult with that apparel in Etambeng. Ngii's attire was all embracing. It reflected a little bit of every cult in Etambeng. It was strange but that did not bother the people.

When they got to the chief's House, he got his young colt that nobody had ridden on before, and adorned it with princely regalia. Then *Sango* Bwemine, *Sango* Nyame Ngole and *Sango* Ngwese Mesape helped Ngii mount the colt. The chief then took the reins himself and led the procession through the cheering crowd to Esam. The men of Etambeng placed palm fronds on the path and women and children threw flowers at the Ngii. It was wonderful. When they got to Esam, the chief, *Sango* Bwemine, *Sango* Ngwese Mesape and *Sango* Nyame Ngole entered the newly built shrine and placed Ngii's container in the shine and immediately they did so a cock crew thrice. They then emerged from the shrine beaming with delight. Esam echoed in shouts of joy. After about fifteen minutes of uncontrolled glamour, *Sango* Ngwese Mesape hushed the crowd to silence. Ngii climbed on a table that had been set in the middle of the courtyard. He thanked the people for the sacrifices they had made on him and his family. He accepted wholeheartedly the powers they had conferred on him and promised to use them as they had assigned them to him. After that he called on his people to entertain the village. Papa, I have never seen such abundance. Even gluttons like *Sango* Epesse could not eat and drink beyond human capacities.

Sango Nkwel'Ngole

Thank you my son. What you have said has mesmerized me. In fact, I don't know how to react. I don't know whether I should laugh, cry or do the two at the same time. It is bad to have a beehive of fools around one. Anyway, our people say, a crab is killed with its own pincers. Even *Sango* Nyame Ngole whom I thought reasoned an inch above the others has failed to see the chasm into which they have led the village. Thank you.

Two days after the investiture of powers, I saw *Sango* Nyame Ngole and *Sango* Bwemine coming towards my house. Since I was singing a lullaby for my grandson to lure him to sleep, I could not feign great pains in my leg to ward them off. I shook my head as they came towards me, sat down on stones and started a conversation.

Sango Nyame Ngole

A Sango Nkwel'Ngol', our people say, even dirty water quenches fire. We are the dirty water. We are sent here to quench your anger. You might have been told how the investiture of powers was carried out. I pointed out that the occasion could not be considered complete until it received your blessing. That is why we are here to tell you to reconsider your stand and join us in the investiture of powers on Epoge.

Sango Nkwel'Ngole

Which is the most powerful animal in the forest? I asked.

Sango Bwemine

Ngii. (The lion).

Sango Nkwel'Ngole

Do you think then that after one has been lionized, he needs any other lionization? Don't you think that tampering with what has already been done would tantamount to adulterating and therefore degrading the perfect? Or have you come to snub me for failing to thwart the investiture?

Sango Nyame Ngole
A Sango Nkwel', we have not reasoned it that way. You know yourself that a person who carries half a jog of water wobbles in movement. Only eight kin groups have administered the investiture. One kin group, your kin group has not participated. So, everything is still hanging in the balance. We need you. And Epoge has promised that he would compensate you heavily if you add your blessing onto those of the other kin groups.

Sango Nkwel'Ngole
So that this cursed clubfoot-sore can heal?

Sango Bwemine
A Sango Nkwel', you did not buy that misfortune and nobody can rebuff you for it. So, don't make a joke of it yourself.

Sango Nkwel'Ngole
I am not making a joke of it. It's another way of saying that I can never barter this painful clubfoot with installing Epoge at Esam. Go and tell those who have sent you that I am adamant.

Sango Nyame Ngole
A Sango, those are the stiff words of a real man.

The Witness
Sango Bwemine and *Sango* Nyame Ngole left *Sango* Nkwel'Ngole in anger. They thought he had treated them shabbily and disdainfully. They could not understand why he was so opposed to Epoge's installation at Esam. When they

got to the chief, they told him in bitter terms, to ostracise him from all other manifestations in the village. As such, the chief slammed his doors against *Sango* Nkwel'Ngole.

Two months after the investiture of powers, *Sango* Nkwel'Ngole heard music all night long emanating from Esam. The project had been realized. Etambeng had a bar of its own. Ngii was at work. The people of Etambeng danced non-stop night after night. The very loud music, coupled with increased pains worked on *Sango* Nkwel'Ngole's nerves. For several days he could not sleep. His wife saw him emaciating and advised that they seek medical intervention. He had in several occasions turned down the idea in fear of amputation. But now, caught in a web of unacceptable conditions, he accepted and within a few days they set off for the Mile One Hospital in Victoria.

Three weeks after their departure, Ngii sent invitations out for the inauguration of the bar. The Senior Divisional Officer of Kumba was invited to carry out the inauguration himself. Because of that high profile personality, dignitaries from Kumba and natives from neighbouring villages heavily attended the inauguration.

Ngii had set the stage. Two weeks before the occasion, the people of Etambeng were made to clear all the roads linking the different quarters or Houses. They raked and burnt the grass to make way for the growth of beautiful young shoots. By the day of the ceremony, Etambeng was sparkling.

The ceremonial ground was arranged according to strict protocol. The administrative tables were on a raised platform overlooking the tables of the nine House-heads of Etambeng, the tables of the chiefs of other villages and last, the tables of the people of Etambeng and their guests.

In receiving the SDO and his entourage the people of Etambeng and their House-heads lined the road to the ceremonial ground in the order in which they had conferred powers on Ngii. Thus, Ngii found himself at the first position and so took up the task of introducing the other dignitaries of the village to the SDO and his entourage.

The House-heads and chiefs from other villages were dressed in identical traditional regalia but Ngii's multicoloured regalia gave him an exotic aura that filled his beholders with awe. That coupled with his prime of place set the stage for the unexpected.

"I am Ngii," *Sango* Ngii introduced himself to the SDO. "I am the newly installed tenth House-head of Etambeng and pivot of this gathering. You are welcome," Ngii concluded with a bow. The SDO nodded his response and appreciation, stretched his hand and shook hands with him. After that, Ngii introduced the rest of the dignitaries. "This is chief Mukete, House-head of Meliog and, custodian of our collective traditional values; This is *Sango* Nyame Ngole, House-head of the House of Muanyam, he is in charge of *ekom*; This is *Sango* Ngwese Mesape, House-head of Nkong, he is in charge of the cult of *mpal*; This is *Sango* Bwemine, House-head of the House of Bwese, he is in charge of the village shrine; This is *Sango* Nnange Mbwoge, House-head of Nnang, he is in charge of the *esue* cult; This is *Sango* Ekem'bepie, House-head of the House of Ekeme, he is in charge of the *mal* cult; This is *Sango* Ngwene'bong, House-head of Muhum, he is in charge of *ahon* cult; This is *Sango* Atume Nguse, House-head of the House of Nyed, he incarnates *Muankum* in this village. Last but not the least; this is the village crier, MC of this occasion to whom I now hand over the floor."

After shaking hands with the dignitaries, the SDO moved to his seat to listen to the MC's brief history of their struggle to liberate Etambeng from the stranglehold of Etaku. He said they were elated that their dream had come true. He thanked the SDO for coming to inaugurate the edifice in person. After saying that, he introduced *Sango* Ngii as the brain behind the ceremony and asked him to welcome the guests.

Sango Ngii stood up, bowed to the SDO, the House-heads of Etambeng, chiefs from other villages and the people of Etambeng and their guests. And in a very brief speech, thanked and welcomed them for attending the occasion. He emphasized that the success of the project was not his alone, but that of all his people, the people of Etambeng. "My people and I worked relentlessly to achieve what is before you," he said with a gape and bow pregnant with expectations.

The MC then invited the SDO to inaugurate the edifice by cutting the tape. He got up with a telling gesture – a sign of the recognition of a wonderful achievement.

The SDO fixed his eyes on Ngii as he moved forth to cut the tape. Before he cut the tape he addressed the attendees.

The SDO

Chief, House-heads and people of Etambeng, invitees, it is with great honour that I come here today to inaugurate this edifice. Your endeavour for self-development is proverbial. It is wonderful that a village like this can achieve this fit with its meagre means. I am proud to be here with you. I am elated to share in your happiness and I tell you most heartily that I shall communicate my feelings, my desire for more development projects in this village to my superiors.

But before that happens, let me tell you that your cry for recognition as an independent village has at last received the attention of the administration. The Governor has asked me to announce to you that from today, your village shall no longer be regarded as an appendage of Etaku. Your chiefdom has been raised to a second class chiefdom. Therefore in inaugurating this bar, I am also inaugurating the new status of your village. Each and everyone of you should as from today know that your village has undergone a metamorphosis that is proverbial. Things will never be the same in this village again. You are liberated. You are free. Make good use of your freedom and let nothing hinder you from enjoying your hard won independence from Etaku.

The Witness
Etambeng exploded in wild applause. For five minutes, the MC tried to put things under control.

The SDO
Your freedom has been achieved by this young, dynamic, patriotic, intelligent, highly educated and self-sacrificing and risk-taking man, Mr. Ngii. I hear you had the foresight of blessing him with your traditional rites. Congratulations for that foresight. Permit me therefore to add to what you have done the administrative blessings our illustrious Head of State conferred on me. Mr. Ngii, be blessed. Receive the powers of command and development and be a symbol of unity, love, peace and progress in this village. I ask all the people of Etambeng to rally behind you. In giving you traditional blessings they chose to move forward with you. You have demonstrated your qualities of good leadership by accomplishing this task. There are many more tasks ahead. Your people need pipe borne water, electricity, educational institutions, health institutions, agricultural posts, you name them. To achieve these, your people should demonstrate their qualities of good stewardship by supporting you in the daunting tasks ahead. This is not the time for sterile and archaic leadership. This is the time for enlightened and onward movement, a time you can record every iota of achievement you make. Our illustrious Head of State himself does not waste words in recognizing great achievements. He simply says, "*Un seul mot, continue*". I would say the same – One single word, **continue**. Continue to build bars, continue to enjoy yourselves, continue to develop your village. Love one another. Forget the past and look forward.

On behalf of the Head of State, and the powers conferred on me, I inaugurate this edifice with the name, **El Do rado** and coffer the rank of **Second Class Chief** on your chiefdom.

Long live our illustrious Head of State, long live the second class chiefdom of Etambeng, long live the Republic of Ekuteng.

The Witness

The SDO cut the tape, raised the scissors, and the ceremonial grounds echoed in ululations and shrieks of jubilation. Before he could move back to his seat, he and *Sango* Ngii were swept off their feet and carried shoulder high by a jubilant population. For ten minutes Etambeng echoed in song and dance, singing the praises of the SDO and Ngii.

It took the MC ten minutes to bring the occasion under control. When he succeeded, he advised the attendees to keep to their seats and wait for entertainment there. Presently, the hostesses brought in food and drinks. The abundance neutralized even gluttons. After the feasting, the SDO and his entourage were given envelopes. *Sango* Ngii gave the SDO a cow while the village gave him six goats and two pigs.

The SDO and his entourage returned full of praises for the people of Etambeng especially, *Sango* Ngii. Immediately the last vehicle left, the people of Etaku who were about a third of the population stood up and returned en masse thus greatly reducing the fanfare. The Etambeng people took their return as a rebuff. They had thought of impressing Etaku population with food and drinks, to show them that Etambeng was a village to reckon with. But now, the people were gone and there were so many leftovers. Etambeng exploded in what it would be in the next fifty years. The sons and daughters of a liberated village sang and danced patriotic songs and dances, hailing the leaders of the new order.

For the first three days after the inauguration, the people saw no need returning to their houses. They recycled the leftovers several times and as they ate, so did they drink. Chief Mukete shuttled between his royal palace and Esam. On the fourth day however, his first wife *Nyango* Esung Mechane, who had been seething with anger at the pronouncements of the SDO, called him and asked him whether he had understood what the SDO meant? She pointed out that by implication the SDO had dismissed him as chief of Etambeng and appointed Ngii in his place. Chief Mukete responded that he and Ngii were not two different persons. He said categorically that Ngii was a son in whom he was well pleased. *Nyango* Esung Mechane went red and scolded him and asked him to order the people to return to their respective homes and resume normal life. He reluctantly asked the village crier to summon his people to the grove. The village crier thought the people won't heed to an ordinary summons. So, he used the *Muankum* drum and invited all and sundry to the grove the next morning. The people obeyed the call and next morning all were there at the grove.

Chapter Seven

Chief Mukete

My people, we have every reason to celebrate the inauguration of El Do rado. But I don't think we are doing it in the proper way. We have virtually abandoned our houses and for four days running, we have lived on the bounty of Esam. This is not bad. But I would want to say that we need to readjust ourselves and face our new realities. If we listened to the SDO very well, he said this village has a new status. Although he said he was making a joint inauguration of the bar and the new status of our beloved village, I believe we have to give more significance to that new status by inviting him and dignitaries from our Provincial capital to come and inaugurate the new status. I would consider what he said, speaking with water in the mouth. It is imperative for him to speak with a clear mouth – that is, tell us about the new status in the presence of people of substance and give us working documents. That is why I have called you to ask you to return to your respective houses and get ready for a more elaborate inauguration in future.

Ngalame

Sango chief, you sound like *Sango* Nkwel'Ngole. You want to undo what we have built. Do you want to cut short the celebration of our hard fought battle against Etaku dominance? I am looking forward to two weeks non-stop celebrations. Esam has not complained that it is exhausted. Our beloved Ngii is ready to provide for us. So, what is your concern?

Dr. Ebule

I believe the chief is right. I have observed with disgust the abuse we are making. People don't go to work in their farms any more, children don't go to school and nobody cares where their family members pass the nights. That is not correct. I think what the chief wants us to do is to be constructive while enjoying ourselves. The English man says, 'All play without work makes Jack a lazy boy'. Laziness is destructive. I would suggest that we lay down rules on how our new realities should be handled. Once we do that, and abide by the rules, everything would be fine.

Nkede

That is echoing *Sango* Nkwel'Ngole. To lay down rules and abide by them is to fetter the people. People must be free in all totality. Independence means freedom.

Etone

Brothers and sisters, our people say, a leaf does not remain on a tree forever. With age it withers and drops. I believe we shall not remain at Esam indefinitely. When we shall be tired we shall go home. Even if we don't get tired, no matter how small a leak is, it empties a tank. So let's leave the dustbin fire smoulder to its end.

The Witness

Etambeng adopted Etone's advice. After the meeting, most of the people went back to the bar. A few went to see what had become of their houses after a four day absence. In nearly all the cases, they were greeted by the combined smells of decaying contents of overturned dustbins, unwashed utensils and chicken and goat droppings. They thus stayed behind to tidy up. Those who did not care and remained at the bar continued the feasting. Although *Sango* Ngii did not manifest overt anger at what was happening, his servants did. They had recycled the leftover food several times and thought it was no longer fit for human consumption. But *Sango* Ngii had no choice but to ask them to recondition the food with maggi and serve the people who were willing to eat it. The maggi gave the swine feed a new taste and the people ate it with revamped appetite.

While they ate, there was a smouldering rumour that *Sango* Nkwel'Ngole had died in hospital while undergoing the amputation of his leg. The man who brought the news said he saw the corpse himself but had no time to inquire whether it would be brought to the village or would be buried in Victoria.

An elated *Sango* Ngii broke the news to all and sundry. Etambeng went wild with jubilation. People did shuttle runs, clapped hands over their heads and ululated to congratulate *Sango* Ngii and chief Mukete. *Sango* Ngii dashed into his stores to see if the drinks would suffice another day of feasting. They couldn't. The stores were almost empty. He at once sent for a lorry load of assorted drinks from Etaku and the feasting started all over again.

Not only drinks were finished. Petrol too was finished. Unfortunately in sending for drinks, Ngii forgot sending for petrol. By midnight, the generators ran out of petrol. It was late to send for petrol and so the dancing stopped. The people of nearby compounds returned home but those whose compounds were far decided to pass the night in the bar.

At about 2.00 a.m. *Nyango* Mesame was woken up by a dart of pain in her stomach. The pain subsided as quickly as it came. She brushed it aside and lay down again to sleep. Just when she was about to doze off she heard the woman lying next to her groan. The woman stood up, held her stomach and wriggled in pains. *Nyango* Mesinze asked what the matter was. Before the woman could respond *Nyango* Mesame yelled as her stomach rumbled in massed pains that slit through her bowels. She curved in, and holding her stomach with both hands, tried to dash out of the dark building to release raging vomit in her throat. She stumbled on some women, lost control and let go. In one long eruption she splattered vomit on the women lying in her path.

The smell and grime of vomit jolted the women from sleep. They cursed, insulted and sighed. *Nyango* Mesinze pleaded with them to open the door. They bumped into each other to open the door. *Nyango* Mesame dashed out and after stepping on a number of puddles of vomit and faeces left behind by earlier victims of the malaise, she sprawled to the ground to empty her bowels through the mouth and anus. The other woman followed her. Half way out of the building she let go an avalanche of vomit. She screamed and called for help. None came. Most of the women, children and a few men were in her situation - suffering from excruciating stomach pains, vomiting and defecating.

The extent of the malaise unfolded in the morning. Not only the people were in a mess, the surroundings too were. Some patients had vomited against the walls of the wooden building and the vomit trapped in-between the joints in the planks was dripping and staining the white wall like thick greasy engine oil. It was a terrible nauseating sight. Women, men and children lay in pools of vomit mixed with faeces like dead fish in an oil spill.

Sango Ngii took the damned situation for a multifaceted ill omen that had to be nipped in the bud. Several things were at stake. If anything uncanny happened it would be taken for the ineffectiveness of powers he had acquired from the House-heads of Etambeng. And *Sango* Nkwel'Ngole's House would go rejoicing that the gods of Esam were avenging themselves. So, though stunned *Sango* Ngii was not frightened. He thought things over quickly and took the ideal action. He ordered his vehicle to take the patients to Etaku dispensary. It made three trips. The dispensary attendants acted promptly and by evening most of the bad cases started responding to treatment. *Sango* Ngii shouldered all the bills and in two days the patients joyfully returned home.

Sango Ngii's magnanimity in handling the food poisoning situation endeared him to the people. They coined a new name for him – Saviour. The name took root quickly and by the time *Sango* Nkwel'Ngole returned from hospital two years later, Etambeng had forgotten the name Ngii. Etambeng had forgotten that the man they referred to as Saviour at the time, was once known as Epoge and later on as Ngii. Saviour had delivered them from the stranglehold of Etaku and from a catastrophe.

Sango Nkwel'Ngole returned from hospital and was stunned to find Etambeng still celebrating the opening of the bar. He called his son Ebune in high pitch. Ebune ran to answer the call.

Sango Nkwel'Ngole
Ebun', Etambeng is still going on with this buffoonery? There has been music non-stop at Esam ever since I returned and from every indication people have been dancing non-stop also. What the hell is wrong with them?

Ebune
They will not call it buffoonery. They will say it is giving honour to where honour is due. They are in fact, adoring the Saviour for building the bar, for having the administration recognize the independence of Etambeng and for saving them from a calamity that would have annihilated the whole village.

Sango Nkwel'Ngole
Fine. I congratulate them. But is that how they are going to go on? Where have they ever heard that dancing and merrymaking bring prosperity to a people? There is the

67

proverb that, 'If you want your dreams to come true, don't sleep'. Don't sleep does not mean, staying awake dancing. It means, staying awake working. So, they should have been working instead of dancing. Ever since Epoge built the bar, how many other people have emulated him and built bars? If the building of bars and drinking of alcohol were development can you call the non-emulation of Epoge progress? Is one plus zero progress? Bars would have been cropping up all over the place by now if they knew what they were doing. Etambeng is blundering. I know most of their farms have overgrown into forests by now. Yes they have. Wine and dance are not good bed mates of the brain. They destroy reasoning. A people deprived of the power of reasoning plunge themselves irretrievably into chasms.

Ebune
Papa, Epoge is now known as Saviour. For some time now, everybody addresses him Saviour.

Sango **Nkwel'Ngole**
Is that how even House-heads address him?

Ebune
Yes. Even chief Mukete himself.

Sango **Nkwel'Ngole**
I think I made a mistake to return. I should have waited for my artificial leg in Victoria. After amputating my leg, the Doctor ordered for a special artificial leg for me. But because he said it would take about four months to come, I decided to return to see how you are faring on with the children. I forgot the other side of Etambeng – the stupidity of the people. You call an intruding stranger Saviour, for saving you from what? For building a bar that would ruin all that your forefathers stood for? Horrible!

Ebune

I have told you why the people are so mad about their Saviour.

Sango Nkwel'Ngole

They leap from one blunder to another. So, every time they have a calamity and somebody redeems them from it the person becomes a saviour. Wowo! It would have been better if I had died. I am saying as if I am not dead? For sure, I am. Any person who is being piecemealed and parts buried in places is dead. Isn't my leg buried in Victoria? Furthermore, Ebun', can you tell me that ever since I returned, it is almost two weeks now, that *Sango* Bwemine and *Sango* Nyame Ngole have not heard that I have returned with half a leg – that my leg was amputated? Isn't that death worthy of condolence? Or to them, death is only when the corpse closes its eyes. I am a living corpse, a corpse with opened eyes. I am surprised that none of them has turned up to console me.

Ebune

If they had come to console you, they would have been taken for switching loyalty and would have lost favour with the Saviour. And who on earth would want to lose favour with benevolence? The whole village looks onto the Saviour for subsistence. More so, most people believe you are an impediment to progress and say if you were here they would not have achieved what they have achieved. As such, they prefer you dead. There was great jubilation during the ceremonies when they heard that you had died in hospital.

Sango Nkwel'Ngole

And so they celebrated my death before hand. That is horrible. What about chief Mukete? How did he react? What about my friends *Sango* Bwemine and *Sango* Nyame Ngole?

Ebune
None of them showed genuine remorse. Their exclamations and expressions of shock lacked depth.

The Witness
Sango Nkwel'Ngole eddied in disbelief and went limp with hate. He X-rayed his relationship with his people. He had always criticised them from the standpoint of love and protection, in other words, criticizing them for their own good – to make them more cautious in taking decisions. He had never wished them evil, but then, there was their reaction towards him – they wished him dead. A hot feeling of revenge built up in him like pus in a boil subjecting him to intermittent starts. He sniggered and made a forecast.

Sango Nkwel'Ngole
I shall celebrate the death of each and everyone of them. They will see. They will die before my eyes and I shall bury them.

Chapter Eight

The Witness

Sango Nkwel'Ngole thought that the best way he would make good his forecast was withdrawing from the worries of Etambeng. He decided to concentrate on his health and his immediate family. With his leg amputated, he was free from pains. And if he had the artificial leg and could move about on his own without bothering sending his grandchildren to help bring things to him he would live a more fulfilling life. So, one month later he left for Victoria for the leg. It arrived two weeks later and for two months he was taught how to use it. By the time he returned to Etambeng he had mastered walking with it with only a slight, virtually imperceptible gait. He was slow quite alright but that did not matter. The leg gave him an appreciable independence and as expected, relieved his children and grandchildren from incessant calls for help. Although he could now move about, he never visited people nor invited them. He stayed in his compound, taking pleasure in tending his livestock and repairing his thatched roofed houses.

After two years of that self imposed seclusion, he started feeling the pinch of isolation. He had gotten used to the buzz and hum of music and noise that came from El Do rado. He had accepted them as an inevitable feature of Etambeng. But as time went on, the monotony was being interrupted by irregular pauses and stoppages, and sometimes days of quiet. That worked on him and he began to have interest in inquiring what the matter was. One day he called his son Ebune and inquired.

Sango Nkwel'Ngole
Ebun', I know you don't often go to El Do rado. But you are more exposed to knowing what is happening there than I am. For two days running I have heard no music at Esam. The whole place seems dead. What is happening? Has the Etambeng population decided to work instead of dancing? Or are the alphas and the omegas of Etambeng getting out of steam?

Ebune
Papa, last Sunday, there was a big fight at El Do rado. They say, when the children of Esam saw the children of the House of Nnang dancing in the middle of the hall, they tried to push them to the corner saying that the centre was the reserve of the children of Esam. The children of the House of Nnang resisted and were backed by the children of the Houses of Mekong and Mehum who had earlier been subjected to the same humiliation. When the children of Esam saw the overwhelming power of the three Houses, they ordered their operator to stop the music. That is why there is no music there. Chief Mukete has convened a meeting on Wednesday to discuss several related cases.

Sango Nkwel'Ngole
Before last Sunday, I head shouts and cries at the House of Bwese. What went wrong?

Ebune
Seh Mesape caught Mr. Okore sleeping with Ebane his sister in his house. He and his children nearly killed Mr. Okore.

Sango Nkwel'Ngole
Why should Mesape and his children beat an epitome of progress? Isn't sleeping with loose women an element of development? Furthermore why is Ebane here? Is she not married at Etaku anymore?

Ebune

Most Etambeng girls that were married at Etaku divorced and came back shortly after the inauguration of the bar. The Saviour refunded their bride price to their former husbands. Even Nzange, my half sister is here. It may be she is avoiding you because she fears you would reprimand her for abandoning her husband and children.

The Witness

Sango Nkwel'Ngole grinned and puckered his face in disgust. He half shut his right eye and tended to have a tunnel-vision of the future of Etambeng with the left eye. After a brief while, an uneasy quiet settled on him and he reminded his son about the meeting on Wednesday. On Wednesday morning it rained so heavily that he thought the meeting would be postponed. He was however surprised when Ebune got an umbrella and jumped into the rain to attend the meeting. Upon his return he asked him whether they had built canopies in the grove. Ebune responded that when the bar was inaugurated the Senior Divisional Officer made pronouncements that compromised the powers of chief Mukete and gave the Saviour undefined powers and privileges. Ever since then village meetings and even *ndies* take place in the bar. He then went on to tell his father how the meeting went on.

Ebune

The meeting started with a four point agenda – the impending SDO's visit, the irresponsible sales of farms and livestock, the behaviour of the children of Esam and *Seh* Mesape's case.

On the issue of the SDO's visit, chief Mukete read the itinerary of the SDO's visit to the Divisional Headquarters in Fangem, and stoppages he would make in major villages along his route to Fangem with a special stoppage at

Etambeng to see the progress the village has made ever since it was elevated to a second class chiefdom. The House-heads of Etambeng were flabbergasted by what they were told. Each made self-examination. There was an unexpected silence. At last *Sango* Nnange Mbwoge stood up with a little growth of anger which he tried to control through a series of throat clearing coughs. He suggested that the village crier be asked to beat the *Muankum* drum immediately asking everybody to clean their compounds and announce that there would be a general inter-House path-clearing on Monday. He said if the SDO by any chance happened to make a surprised visit to Etambeng and met the squalid conditions in which the people lived he would faint seeing what Etambeng was when he last came there. He talked of the overgrown inter-House paths, the state of the different Houses, Houses flagged with mud pools with rotting toads, maggots, fleas, mosquitoes and accumulated damp rot. He pointed at the moulding walls of the bar itself, moulding with vomit several days if not weeks old.

On the issue of the sales of farms, *Sango* Bwemine as House-head in charge of the village shrine, condemned the sales of the farm and virgin bush within the periphery of the shrine. He said he heard that the widow who owned the farm sold it but he was not sure whether she was the one who also sold the virgin bush. He added that he had tried to find out to no avail to whom she had sold the farm. *Sango* Atume Nguse picked up from him and said he had heard that it was the Saviour who bought the farm and the sacred vicinity – land bordering a shrine is sacred. He added that most Etambeng people have pledged their farms to the Saviour on 'chop loss' but because of constant renewal of the pledges they have already taken so much money from him that there was no way they could recuperate the farms. Because Etambeng was short of labour, the Saviour has turned to Etaku for farm hands. Most of the land in

Etambeng was being exploited by people of Etaku. Eyalla, a young man from the House of Nyed said he heard that all the grazing hillocks that constitute the border between Etaku and Etambeng have been sold to Etaku herdsmen.

On the issue of the sales of livestock, *Sango* Ngwene'bong said he heard that the Saviour had bought most of the livestock and sent them to his ranch at Etaku. He added that most Etaku people buy livestock from Etambeng through Etambeng agents.

On the issue of the uppishness of the children of Esam, *Sango* Nnange Mbwoge pointed out that the children of Esam had begun behaving like the people of Etaku, and if that continued, he would prefer his children to go to Etaku to be humiliated in having fun, than be humiliated in their own village.

On the issue of Ebane sleeping with a lover in her brother's house, *Sango* Ekem b'Epie picked up from *Sango* Nnange Mbwoge, and said Etambeng had become a promiscuous village. Wives slept outside. Husbands sold farms to drink beer. Children didn't go to school. The moral decadence of Etambeng was unprecedented anywhere. The village wore the crown of the most promiscuous village in the world.

These revelations did not work well on the Saviour. He got up in a rather subdued manner and seized the floor from the last speaker.

He said he believed there was mudslinging amongst the people of Etambeng that would set the village ablaze. If what was said against him and his collaborators was true, the people of Etambeng should show proof. To help the carriers of rumours do so, he suggested that the meeting be adjourned.

Although he spoke as if he was asking for a favour, the Etambeng people took it for what it was – a decree adjourning the meeting. They had no choice but to comply.

They complied anticipating some sort of compensation in drinks. But perhaps because the Saviour was hurt he did not provide the drinks. The rain continued unabated. For hours the people waited, drawing their noses and eying beer on the shelves. The Saviour remained adamant; enjoying the pain his decision not to entertain caused the people. When the rain ceased they left El Do rado with a noticeable line of divide between them – those who had dared point out the wrongdoings of the Saviour and those who blamed the loss of his benevolence on the dare-the-devil adventurers.

The Witness

Sango Nkwel'Ngole nearly retched from what he heard. It was disgusting but he could decipher a silver lining in it. He saw crevices in Etambeng society. He knew very soon they would turn into big cracks and erupt into open quarrels. At that time the weaker side would bow onto him for help. He invited *Sango* Nnange Mbwoge to find out how Etambeng was moving.

Sango Nnange Mbwoge

A Sango Nkwel'Ngol', you are a wizard. I wonder whether we can ever reach the depth of your knowledge. I have every reason to believe that you had foreseen what Etambeng is going through today. The chief's eldest wife, *Nyango* Esung Mechane started complaining to me long ago about the gradual erosion of the chief's authority in the village. She said that Ngii was gradually and surely seizing the powers of her husband because under the influence of alcohol, he allowed him chair council sessions in the bar. There was even a rumour that Ngii tried to bribe a House-head who incarnates *Muankum* to turn against the chief. On the issue of where to receive the SDO, Ngii is arguing that because the weather is uncertain in May, El Do rado was the ideal place and not the grove. The majority of people see with him but my question is, hadn't we occasions in the grove before El Do rado was built?

I suggest reconciliation between the two parties. I believe that if the sages of this village put their heads together, the two parties will reconcile. All traditional occasions should be held at the chief's compound or the grove and all modern ones at El Do rado.

The Witness

Sango Nkwel'Ngole reeled in anger and blasted *Sango* Nnange Mbwoge.

Sango Nkwel'Ngole

A Mue Nnange, are you suggesting reconciliation between the chief and the Saviour in order that they share equal rights and powers in this village? Wouldn't that be compromising and relegating the chief to second place? I know you have sold your birthrights and are no longer conscious of the stakes in Etambeng. You are talking of receiving the SDO; is the SDO an ancient or a modern institution? If you think modern occasions should be held at El Do rado, then of course, Epoge is right to insist that the SDO be received in his bar.

Sango Nnange Mbwoge

A Sango Nkwel', all in all, the goings on in Etambeng bloats one's stomach. Sometimes even the sages are stupefied. The other day *Nyango* Mbinze met me and complained that we have bartered chief Mukete's authority with beer. I told her it was the SDO and *Sango* chief himself who have caused the confusion in Etambeng. Chief Mukete washes his face and brushes his teeth in the bar. But for his first wife who is restraining him, he would have moved house. In other not to displease people, I sought reconciliation. That was the best I could do.

77

Sango Nkwel'Ngole

That was the best you could do because you bite the truth. If you did not bite the truth, you would have spoken out the truth. The women of Etambeng say the men have betrayed them. The other day *Nyango* Mbinze came here and told me they have formed an association of Women of Substance to counter the buffoonery of the men. She said they were fighting to impose that the oncoming reception of the SDO takes place in the village grove or in the chief's house and if the SDO did not like it that way, he could go on with Ngii and beer drinkers in the bar without women.

This shows that the chief's wife has a very strong female backing. And if things go on the way she says, there would be hopes of salvaging this village from impending calamities. The women will lead if the men fail. The chief's wife has become very popular and powerful.

The Witness

As Etambeng erupted on where to receive the SDO, there was a radio announcement that the visit had been postponed indefinitely following the abrupt change of the cabinet. In spite of that, Etambeng was split into two factions – people who favoured the occasion to take place in the village grove and those who favoured it to take place in El Do rado. The two factions were at daggers drawn. The tension worsened with each passing day. But gradually, the chief's powerful wife gained grounds. The Saviour saw his influence waning. Even chief Mukete was getting sober. Eight House-heads held regular meetings without inviting the Saviour on how to handle the tension. Although most of them pleaded for caution, there were indications that they were tilting towards chief Mukete.

One evening, a mysterious fog hung over Etambeng for about twenty minutes making breathing very difficult. It was horrible. Children and sick people especially the elderly suffocated and convulsed. Etambeng House-heads asked the village crier to invite the village to the grove the next morning. They wanted to find out the cause of the fog.

As the village prepared for the meeting, they heard cries in chief Mukete's compound. Nobody took the cries seriously. Most people thought a child had convulsed. But when female cries started getting interlaced with male cries, the village rushed to the compound and found the impossible. The chief's wife who was sound and well a few minutes earlier lay dead, dead like a stone. The people asked her daughter what happened.

Mbole (daughter of the deceased)
I was washing pans outside. When I entered the kitchen to put the pans on the table, mama stood up suddenly as if something had hit her. Then she screamed, fell down and ... I don't know. I can't tell. Then blood started coming from her nose.

Nzole (friend of Mbole)
I was in the kitchen with *Neh* Esung Mechane when *Mue* Mbole entered to put the pans on the table. When *Neh* Esung Mechane stood up, I thought she wanted to get the pans from *Mue*. Then I saw her fall down. I did not see what hit her. She just fell down. When *Mue* Mbole started crying I also started crying and people came.

Dielle (co-wife)
When I head Mbole and Nzole crying, I thought they had broken plates. So I took my time to go there. But when I saw Mbole rolling on the ground I dashed into the kitchen and saw the impossible. This is not a natural death. This death must be investigated. I am a woman but I challenge the whole village to react. This death is not for nothing.

The Witness

Most of the villagers thought they had to investigate the cause of death. So, they cut the toe and finger nails and hair of the chief's wife, tied them in a piece of black cloth and sent three boys with them to Echugenyo to find out from the renowned soothsayer, *Sango* Nsunlide, the cause of the death of the chief's wife. This is what they told the aggrieved village upon their return.

1st Emissary

As you all know, we left here on the evening of the death of *Nyeh* Esung Mechane and trekked all night. When we got to Puoala, we rested for about twenty minutes and took off again. We got to Echugenyo next morning, after trekking for two nights and one day non-stop. We asked where the soothsayer's house was. A child was sent to show us the house. The man received us as if he knew that we were coming. His wife gave each of us hot water to bathe and presently offered us food. After eating and thanking the couple for their hospitality, we told the man what had brought us. I started the consultation.

I told him, we had been sent by the village of Etambeng to come and enquire about the death of our chief's wife who died suddenly two days ago. I presented the cut nails and hair of the woman. I told him we have trekked for two nights and one day to get there because we intended to enquire and return to present our findings to the village at the burial. The whole village wanted people to swear on the corpse before it was buried.

Sango Nsunlide

I sensed your arrival. I would have gone to Ejoke. How is your chief himself?

2ⁿᵈ Emissary

His is well but very aggrieved. He does not even eat.

Sango Nsunlide

Why is he very aggrieved, didn't he expect what has happened?

His wife has died in his place because he made her stick out her neck where he would have exercised his prerogatives. He let things slip out of his grip. There is a man in your village that is a primed gun. I see your chief planning revenge. If he tries, he too will go. The man who killed his wife is too powerful. There is nobody apart from one lame man in your village who can dare the man. He killed the chief's wife because she stood on his way. Return to your village and tell your people to accept the death as it has come. Revenge may turn out to be disastrous.

3ʳᵈ Emissary

Can the man be above the combined forces of the whole village? I am asking this because everybody is in sympathy with the chief and they want revenge.

Sango Nsunlide

Your village cannot boast of a combined force. Your village is as light as dry plantain leaves. Only one man, I am afraid, he may not even accept to fight the man I am talking about. Only he and he alone can shake the killer of the chief's wife.

2ⁿᵈ Emissary

What about you? Suppose we ask you to do something, shan't it work? Our people may want to use the combined forces of prominent traditional witchdoctors to revenge the death of our chief's wife

Sango Nsunlide

A mue, when small streams enter a river, they lose every aspect of their individuality. They lose their individual names as their waters become indivisible with the water of the river. The river swells in size and fish life. The river does not say it was once boosted by small streams. It says, "I am," because it is. That is the situation in your village. Anybody who tries to disentangle your situation might end up calling the wrath of your lack of foresight. So, tell your people to accept the death as it has come. Let the chief not attempt revenge. The odds are too much against him.

The Witness

The emissaries returned to Etambeng two days after the burial of *Nyango* Esung Mechane, the chief's wife. No swearing on the corpse was done during the burial because the talismans that were expected from *Sango* Nsunlide had not been brought. The village became even more disappointed when they heard the result of the trip from the 1st emissary.

1st Emissary

We left Echugenyo completely shattered. Our people say, a successful hunting expedition is never tiring but a failed expedition crushes the hunter and he gets bored even with his gun. Ours was a failed expedition and every step we made on our way back was terribly painful. The people of Etambeng are now challenged with interpreting what *Sango* Nsunlide describes as, small streams entering a river and losing their individual names.

Chapter Nine

Sango Nkwel'Ngole

The people of Etambeng were surprised with the way I participated in the burial ceremony of _Nyango_ Esung Mechane. After the burial I went to chief Mukete's compound everyday to participate in the collective mourning. People had thought I was the chief's worst enemy. I wasn't his enemy. I was only against his lack of foresight. The puzzle the emissaries had brought from _Sango_ Nsunlide was there for them to unravel but none of them took interest in it. They could not even draw inferences from the conversation the emissaries had with the soothsayer. As usual, they beat about the bush. Some said that age had caught up with _Sango_ Nsunlide and so he was unable to divine. Others suggested that they send other emissaries to other diviners. All that to me was akin to asking an outsider to tell the insider the hole in the wall that announced daybreak. I counted the years from the time of the investiture of powers to the time of the death of the chief's wife. It was only five years, and Etambeng could not interpret that, that was the time small streams entered the **Ngii River**. I laughed and called _Sango_ Nyame Ngole and asked him what the sages of Etambeng thought about the puzzle.

Sango Nyame Ngole

A Sango Nkwel'Ngol' these are situations that 'fill one's stomach with water'. I am as ignorant as any other person is. The chief himself is confused. But I think _Sango_ Bwemine and _Sango_ Atume Nguse are trying to put their heads together e, e, e, e.

The Witness

Sango Nkwel'Ngole eyed *Sango* Nyame Ngole contemptuously and sighed. He stood up to return to his house. When the chief's young wife Nzange, saw him going, she called him back and offered him food. He refused eating. He said his mouth was sour but to show good faith he carried the food home. In the evening, *Nye* Mengongu, his wife who, like most other friends of the deceased spent the nights at the home of the deceased, returned to see how *Sango* Nkwel'Ngole was faring on with the children. She told him that she had eavesdropped on the chief's conversation with some of his trusted House-heads and this is what they said.

Chief Mukete

A Sango Ekem'bepie, *Sango* Nnange'Mbwoge, *Sango* Bwemine and *Sango* Nyame Ngole, you are the House-heads in this village who know how I sleep. In other words, you are the ones who are very close to me and in whom I confide everything. I need not tell you that I am dead. You have heard of my death. You have participated in the mourning. But you should know now that I am dead. It is not Mekoge's mother who is dead. It is me. Me. I am the one who is dead.

So, I have called you together for us to reason out a way to avenge my wife's death. That is what has made me call you. Our people say, a river with no tributaries winds. You are my tributaries.

Sango Ekem'bepie

Sango chief, we all know that you are the one who is dead. A person of your age who loses his first wife is dead. The young girls one marries later in life and shares with young men are not wives. It is the first wife who knows whether one is hungry or not, whether one is constipated or not, or whether one has catarrh or not. Before you called us here we were conferring on what to do to avenge that death. Gossip points at only one direction. I for one had counted on *Sango* Nsunlide. He is a very renowned witchdoctor but I wonder why he says the person responsible for the death of your wife is a rock that cannot be cracked.

Sango Nnange'Mbwoge

A Sango chief, I am still pondering over the puzzle *Sango* Nsunlide sent to us. Whenever I try to juxtapose it with *Sango* Nkwel'Ngole's refusal to have Epoge installed at Esam certain hazy nuances linger in my mind.

But the plain truth is that a borrowed hoe does not complete the weeding. Begged water does not cook a meal. If *Sango* Nsunlide means that because we gave Epoge our individual House powers in a collective ceremony, Epoge has become the river into which we have lost our identity, I must say, he who begs hasn't the same power as he who owns. We owned the powers we ceded to him. We can withdraw them as we ceded to him. If it is Epoge who has killed your wife because she challenged him, then he is as good as dead himself. I would like us to incorporate *Sango* Nkwel'Ngole in whatever plans we are making. Thank God he is doing well. His leg that used to worry him is healed and I believe he will be more open and constructive now.

Chief Mukete

If we want any success in this thing we should not mention the name Nkwel'Ngole. He will dismantle all we try to build.

Sango Nyame Ngole

I believe *Sango* Nnange Mbwoge's inferences are an eye-opener. I have faith in what he has said. He, who is given, cannot have more power than he who gave. The person we gave powers cannot be more powerful than us. So I propose that *Sango* chief should assemble his village in the grove and ask the House-heads to withdraw the powers they had bestowed on Epoge. Once he is stripped of the powers, even a virgin can blow him out of this planet.

Chief Mukete

A Banyang, I thank you very much for the concern you have shown in the death of my wife. Our people say, nobody teaches another person how to cry his mother. Nobody will teach me how to cry *Nyeh* Mekoge. I shall cry her rolling in dust, I shall cry her rolling in mud, I shall cry her in the dry season, and I shall cry her in the raining season. Before I called you, I had had an intimate conversation with my maternal uncles. They told me about a man at Ekite. They said the man does not waste time when it comes to avenging situations like mine. They have promised to take me to him tomorrow. While away, I shall want you to go on with your plans. We have all heard that the man is a rock. So we should not attack him only from one front. Prepare to carry out the collective withdrawal of the powers we conferred on him. Thank you.

Sango Nkwel'Ngole

Nyeh Mengongu's near verbatim report filled me with awe for her. She is fantastic in verbatim reporting. *Sango* Nsunlide had warned against attacking the person who had killed the chief's wife because the consequences would be disastrous. Now, the chief and his maternal uncles were planning to attack. Furthermore, the chief's close House-heads were planning to withdraw the powers they had bestowed on the new House-head of Esam. For sure, there was a storm in the making in Etambeng. So long as I was concerned, I would watch and see. After all, I was ostracized.

About three months after the burial of the chief's wife, my wife heard cries from Esam. She woke me up and said she suspected something serious had happened at Esam. We listened attentively. After a while she said it was Epoge's first wife who was crying. She cried:

Nkumbe mme mbweme nziog mwene mmbode. (The gun that shot the elephant has itself exploded. This meant that the person who killed the human elephant (the Queen) has been killed)

I wondered whether Epoge (who was the main suspect in the death of the chief's wife) was dead. If so, then the chief and his maternal uncles deserved a pat on the back. The cries intensified and we all rushed to Esam. We met Epoge in a bad state but not life-threatening. He was breathing and sweating heavily. I looked at him and pouted. There was evidence that he was shot with *ngalemudumbu* – a very powerful one, but because he was well fortified the pellets could not penetrate and do the required damage in him.

"O!" I exclaimed. "Stupidity is worse than smallpox. If this fool (chief Mukete) knew he wouldn't put an end to this fellow why did he attempt?" I inwardly asked myself, sighed and shook my head. I predicted that Epoge would unleash a devastating counterattack once he got well. He was rushed to Muamedom for treatment and after two weeks he returned completely cured.

Upon his returned, the chief's close collaborators were panicky and convened a meeting in the grove for the withdrawal of Epoge's powers. Epoge overheard the plot and did not wait. He countered by aiming at the chief. *Boooom*, he shot him with a light but punishing volley of *ngalemudumbu*. The chief fell suddenly sick – stricken by life-threatening mbim (swollen stomach). Mekoge take note. That was the first time your father was taken to Kodmin for treatment. He remained there for a very long time. In fact most people forgot about him.

Chapter Ten

The Witness

People forgot about chief Mukete because soon after the inauguration of the bar, he virtually ceded his powers to Epoge whom he called son. Although Epoge was inspired by the SDO's pronouncements he was cautious and tactful. He did not go in for open confrontation. He lay in wait like a python and used his bar as a weapon. Within a short time, he succeeded in making the people addicted to alcohol. And being addicted, they simply thought whatever he said and did was good. Only chief Mukete's late wife had detected the intrigues and time and again challenged him. Now, with her death and chief Mukete's absence Epoge saw a rear opportunity and capitalized on it. He convened an impromptu meeting in his bar and invited all the House-heads including *Sango* Nkwel'Ngole. *Sango* Nkwel'Ngole sent his son Ebune to represent him.

Sango Ngii

People of Etambeng, we are all aware that our beloved chief Mukete is not well and that he is receiving treatment at Kodmin. We all are concerned with the misfortunes that have befallen him of late. We all wish him speedy recovery. In wishing him quick recovery, we cannot sit with folded arms waiting. We have to work to develop this village. You all heard what the SDO said some years ago on the day he inaugurated El Do rado. He said these were not the times for sterile traditional leadership. He wished that we follow the modern approach to development. We cannot do so with traditional structures in place. Traditional structures hinder development because they are closed systems. We need open systems – those in which any of us who are capable can be made to lead the people within a specified time. In that case the best brain of a given period leads the people to progress and when the time comes, another best brain is chosen. Thus power moves from one dynamic hand to another.

In the traditional set-up, whether somebody is intellectually fit or not, so long as he is an offshoot of the ruling family, he is made to lead. So you see, power has remained in the same hands for eternity. That does not bring development. I see in each and every one of you the potential for leadership. But under the traditional system, you are condemned never to lead. That injustice has to end. I am therefore calling on you to exercise your inalienable rights, rights God created you with to help replace the system of hereditary chieftaincy and House-headship. Those who agree with me should indicate with a show of hand.

The Witness

Nine-tenths of the hall raised their hands. Only the original House-heads who now looked desperate and a few elderly persons did not. Because the meeting was heavily attended Ngii took that as an overwhelming victory.

He entertained the participants heavily and then went on to make new structures for Etambeng. He dismantled the original House-headship and created what he called Compound-headship. Each original House was split into two unequal independent Compounds, with the original House-head given the smaller Compound. Thus there were thirty one Compounds – Esam having been split into three Compounds. Ngii abrogated hereditary posts and replaced them with electoral ones. Thus the chief was to be elected by an electoral college of Compound-heads and compound-heads by people of the Compound. Before the election, he appointed twenty one new Compound-heads. He banned the holding of occasions in the village grove and changed the leadership of the most prominent cults of the village. The new cult leaders had a casting vote for every contested election result. The cult of *Muankum* the most powerful cult in the tribe, the cult in charge of maintaining law and order, he gave to his brother *Sango* Elondo of the 1st Compound of Esam, the cult of *Ahon*, the richest and most noble cult, he gave to his half brother of the 2nd Compound of Esam, and the cult of *mmpal*, the most lucrative, he gave to his son of the 3rd Compound of Esam.

He then announced that there would be chieftaincy and Compound-headship twin elections in two weeks; two weeks to give potential contestants enough time to file in their candidatures and carry out campaign. He instituted an electoral fee for each of the posts – one elephant, two buffaloes and two hogs for those contesting for the chieftaincy post, and one buffalo, one hog, two goats for the Compound-head post. He declared his candidacy for the chieftaincy post, paid its fee, and also paid those of his appointed Compound-heads.

When news spread that the village had that abundance in electoral fee, there was no gain say. Ngii was declared winner with a landslide before the elections. He did not waste time. Since no other candidate had access to the *mmpal* cult, none could pay the election fee. The village slaughtered the animals and even the most remote widows received gifts of meat from Ngii. The bar was open for twenty four hours each day.

Ngii instructed *Sango* Elondo to use to the maximum the powers of *Muankum* to keep law and order. While people drank and ate, praise-singers sang his virtues. They sang that he was god incarnate, benevolent, majestic, forgiving, all-knowing, tolerant, magnificent winner of independence for Etambeng and marvellous developer and saviour.

For two weeks no other candidate could raise the election fee. So, Ngii in his magnanimity offered to pay the fee for any candidate who would want to contest. No candidates came forth. So he handpicked twenty contestants amongst his supporters and paid their election fee. The chosen fellows hired praise singers to sing their praises and condemn Ngii. The campaign rhetoric tended to work in favour of the fellows. Things got heated up towards the close of the campaign. On the election-day however, Ngii and his chosen team won with a landslide majority 99.99% and 77.77% respectively. Ngii declared a two week non-stop celebration of their victory.

While he was celebrating his victory, the original House-heads of Etambeng *Sango* Ekem'bepie (Atume's father) *Sango* Nnange 'Mbwoge, (Dione's father), *Sango* Bwemine (Mukala's father) and *Sango* Nyame Ngole (Ngwese's father) held high level secret meetings to counter what they termed, Ngii's wanton destruction of their village set-up. They saw the creation of new structures and the introduction of elections as a provocative and unacceptable move to dispossess them of their inalienable rights. So, they sent emissaries to Kodmin asking chief Mukete to return to Etambeng and reclaim his chieftaincy from what they called an intruder.

Upon his return, chief Mukete convened a meeting in which the House-heads discussed Ngii's usurpation of village powers, destruction of time tested village institutions, illegal seizure of people's farmlands including that of the chief himself, seizure of people's livestock and Ngii's uppishness. They also complained about his arrogance and the extravagance of the members of his family.

After listening to the complaints, Chief Mukete decided to act promptly. He told the aggrieved House-heads to attack Ngii. Ngii got wind of the plot and shot *Sango* Ekem'bepie and *Sango* Nnange'Mbwoge with mild pellets of *ngalemudumbu* to play havoc on them. His aim was to torture them and not to kill them straight. They both suffered from strange mild malaises which doctors could not determine the cause. They grew pale and lost weight. Finally, they were advised to go for traditional treatment in other villages. Atume and Dione were just a few years old when their parents left Etambeng for treatment in other villages. When they got well and returned to Etambeng, Ngii fired the *coup de grace* rounds of *ngalemudumbu* at them. They fell instantly ill again and were forced back to their places of refuge. They both died miserably after years of suffering and were buried there because Ngii wouldn't allow their corpses to be brought home.

Sango Bwemine (Mukala's father) was enraged with the death and burial of prominent Etambeng people out of the village. He challenged Ngii openly accusing him of being responsible for the deaths and burials of Etambeng patriarchs in foreign lands. He warned him that if he continued with the process of eliminating the patriarchs of Etambeng, the surviving people would assemble the whole tribe to try him. Ngii did not take that lightly. He shot *Sango* Bwemine. In his agony, he was advised to seek treatment out of the village. He refused. He said he preferred to die in his village than go and die in another village, and thus give Ngii the cause for making him buried there. He was sick for a long time. When he finally died, he was buried in his compound. That is why his children (Mukala and his brothers and sisters) remained in Etambeng.

As the original House-heads of Etambeng and other prominent people died, their families migrated to other villages. Ngwese's father, *Sango* Nyame-Ngole was shot on Sunday. His family rushed him to the traditional doctor's place at Ebwengo but before he got there, he died. He was buried by the roadside where he died because Ngii forbade people from bringing his corpse home.

It was a terrible experience. The Etambeng women who had divorced their Etaku husbands were the most compromised. They pleaded with their former husbands to be given shelter on humanitarian grounds but were spited.

When the surviving people of Etambeng saw that things were getting worse, they approached *Sango* Nkwel'Ngole and pleaded with him to help stem the tide. He laughed contemptuously at them and asked;

Sango Nkwel'Ngole
Are you teasing me? If you are fleeing from a catastrophe, on whose back will you climb – on the back of an amputee or on that of a wholesome person? A man who once died in hospital cannot be asked to redeem people who drink and make merry.

Sango Abate
A sango Nkwel'Ngole, you are taking it lightly. You are joking. It will soon be our turn, and if we don't act now it would be too late. Ngii is not joking. How many people have died so far? Do you want Ngii to bury all of us before you react?

Sango Nkwel'Ngole
I am not taking it lightly. I am not joking. Who doesn't dread the cutting of heads? If you think you are threatened, then of course, I am threatened. I am as vulnerable and helpless in this situation as you are. Or can you tell me where I draw my powers? You think I can help you stem the tide. I have told you I cannot. The whole thing looks funny.

Sango Abate
Funny! You are joking with a life or death situation? I believe that Ngii wants to wipe-out the old generation in other to create a new generation that would know only about him. In that new situation, he would create new genealogies and thus establish a completely new order in Etambeng.

A Sango Nkwel', if the rest of the people wouldn't fight *Sango* Ngii mystically, I shall fight him physically. I shall use my Dane gun and kill him. I shall kill him even if Buea will hang me for it.

Sango Nkwel'Ngole

Sango Kome bought the idea and the two of them loaded their Dane guns and went to Esam. They shot Ngii four times. The bullets homed in but lodged just below the skin making minor pimple-like blotches on him. He pressed them the way one would press pimples and the bullets dropped on the ground. Ngii gathered them and poked them into their eyes with a sinister folding of the forehead. He grimaced, laughed at them and exhaled. He reeled and fired two devastating rounds of *ngalemudumbu* at them. They got in squarely and paralyzed them on the left side. Where they lay was where they defecated. They soon developed bedsores. Before they died, they were infested with maggots.

Etambeng was in the grip of terror. People fled in their numbers. The only surviving elders were those who had managed to migrate to distant villages beyond the reach of Ngii's *ngalemudumbu*. The children of House-heads were targeted and so they all fled. Chief Mukete moved about with a blank terrified and helpless countenance. According to what Ebune told me, several people pleaded with him to ask me to intervene but he refused. Our people say, a fowl may refuse eating an insect, but if the insect keeps stepping onto its way, it may jump at it and eat it. To avoid getting into the damned situation, I left for Victoria to consult with my Doctor. I was there for three months. On my return, Ebune told me about the confrontation chief Mukete had with Ngii, and the subsequent death of chief Mukete.

Chapter Eleven

Ebune

One evening I went to Esam in search of my missing goat I suspected Ngii might have caught since he was fond of catching people's livestock in the pretext that they had strayed into his property. To my surprise, I met Chief Mukete having a very serious brawl with him right there at Esam. Chief Mukete was furious. There was every indication that he was well prepared for the confrontation. For the first time, I admired him. He spoke with authority and tended to make an impact. He called Ngii a usurping stranger and ordered him out of his village. Chief Ngii didn't take that kindly. He eyed him disdainfully, pouted and told him in a rather low but sinister voice that he, Ngii was the officially elected chief of Etambeng and that the old system had died and was buried. He boasted that he was fully in command. He said he had received the approval of the ancestors and the administration and nothing could shake him.

With that, the tables turned. Chief Mukete got rather confused. It seems as if he did not take the precautions his traditional doctor might have asked him to take under such circumstances. He might not have worn his amulets. So, when Ngii cast a stern stare at him, he became inhibited and lost vitality. I saw him deflate like a balloon with a minute puncture and withdraw from the confrontation rather defeated.

Ngii, dashed into his shrine did some skirmishes with the mystical and I believe, fired the *coup de grace* at him. Chief Mukete was seized by an instant bout of trembling. His second wife, with whom he had come, sent for you. I told her you had travelled to Victoria to consult your Doctor. She thus rushed him back to Kodmin. A few days later we heard that the chief was dead.

The people of Kodmin sent several emissaries to Etambeng requesting the people to come for the corpse of their chief. But perhaps because of the lack of manpower or the refusal of Ngii to allow the corpse in Etambeng, nobody went and so chief Mukete was buried in Kodmin.

The Witness

Chief Mukete's death dispirited the people. Everyday people talked of sending Ebune to Victoria to bring his father. They considered him the only hope. Things got worse everyday. It was horrible. Even those who had migrated did not have it easy. Their ordeal was worse. Those who had migrated to Etaku were virtually slaves there. They did all sorts of mean jobs to live. They were employed (for barely subsistence wages) to recover overgrown farms, sweep compounds, wash corpses and toilets in the Etaku hospital and take care of children going to school. Some elderly people, who could not do all that, became beggars. Those addicted to alcohol but had no money drank the leftover in bars. The worse off were the women who had divorced their Etaku husbands. They were not accepted in any circle. They were spited and derided. Nobody even talked to them. Pushed to the wall, they wrote a joint apology to the chief and people of Etaku asking them to forgive them. They pleaded to be taken back on humanitarian grounds. The chief and his people spat on the letter and grimaced disdainfully at the folly. At the peak of the tragedy, Ebune thought if he had the means, he would have stepped in to rescue the people.

Sango Nkwel'Ngole

To rescue them and win a crucifix? That to me sounds strange. Suppose you give a dog food on a leaf and the dog drags the food onto the ground and when it starts eating it complains that the soiled food is not good, would you, because it is your dog, go and clean the food and put it in its mouth? I have returned. But I can't be drawn into that pugnacity.

Ebune

Papa, dogs, children and the mentally inept cannot be judged on the same latitude as the mentally apt. By this I mean, it is where you forbid dogs, children and the mentally inept not to go for their own safety that they go.

The stories we hear about our people in neighbouring villages are hair-raising. The other day, one man told me that one of our children in Etaku was beaten almost to death when he was suspected of having stolen one hundred francs. When the truth about the money was finally uncovered, the people who beat him apologized. But the child was too aggrieved to forgive them. He preferred to move out of Etaku and resettle in another village. But he did not last long in the village. He died most probably from the after effects of the beating. Every crime that is committed at Etaku is attributed to our children. The people of Etaku exhibit extreme audacity on our people and drive them into crime. It is said six Etaku boys gang-raped one of our girls. The Etaku council dismissed the case on grounds of insufficient evidence. With that apathy, came rancour. But the girl fought back with lethal intrigues. By the time it was discovered that she was behind the deaths of two of her rappers it was too late. She was not only chased out of Etaku as a witch but all the refugees from Etambeng became targets of wanton attacks. Mutual recrimination set in. Etambeng people became persona non grata. And with that, the people set out again to seek asylum in other villages. Even there, their stories are horrifying.

I was told of how one of our boys ignorantly discovered the corpse of a missing hunter in his village of refuge. Instead of being praised he and his poor mother were subjected to an elaborate and expensive cleansing ritual. There is this story of how two of our women (mother and daughter) were chased out of a certain village because the girl would not sleep with the boys of the village. Then there is the story of one of our girls who gave birth in the village of her asylum but could not find a place to bury the afterbirth. The villagers refused showing her a place to bury the afterbirth because they did not want to make the child a citizen of their village. There are so many stories – so many pathetic and annoying stories. Fortunately, I cannot recall all. If I had the means I would have done something. Those people are fleeing from Ngii and nothing else. If I had the means I would do something for them.

Sango Nkwel'Ngole

What do you imply by that? You expect me to attack Ngii? That would be fighting an unjust war. Etambeng people sent somebody to see me immediately I returned from Victoria. When the person came and said they wanted me to intervene in the destruction of Ngii, I told him that I had no problem with Ngii and so could not launch an attack on an innocent person. If I did, I would be calling the wrath of God on me. Now, you are implying the same thing. I cannot attack Ngii until he attacks me. Our people say, a spear launched in anger misses its target.

Ebune

Ngii is now in full control of Etambeng. He owns all the land of Etambeng. He owns all the surviving women. He owns all the livestock. He owns everything. Most of the time, he goes to Etaku to see his ranches. In fact, he spends most of his time at Etaku. He passes by your estate. Since he has insatiable appetite for people's property he may be eying it. So, if you say nothing should be done, fine.

The Witness

One evening I was passing by *Sango* Nkwel'Ngole's house. I realized that his wife was under the spell of something seriously wrong. I asked her what was wrong. She shook her head and indicated that I should leave her alone and go away. I went away. The next morning I went on a journey. I am glad, I am here today to listen to him tell us about Etambeng. I believe he will tell us what happened on that day.

Sango Nkwel'Ngole

One evening, I felt as if something had hit me. I felt as if a metal pellet had hit me and penetrated my body. Before long, I was bleeding in the nose. I told my wife, *Nyeh* Mengongu to take a small black bundle of powder from my *ngwem* and dilute it with *manyanga* and give me. She horridly did so and when she gave me I licked it reciting the names of the ancestors of Etambeng. Then I told her that a chest-pounding gorilla had called the wrath of the ancestors upon itself. She said she did not understand what I meant. I told her that I was struck by a pellet from a well primed *ngalemudumbu* and that by the gods of Etambeng, the person responsible would live to regret. She screamed and thought of going to invite my maternal uncles at Ekiteh village for help. Although I calmed her down and told her that my condition would improve because I had taken a powerful and effective antidote, she was restless. She agitated with suppressed sobs and drew her nose to my dislike.

I knew the man who had fired the *ngalemudumbu* would be expecting cries from my compound very soon. I knew if he did not hear the cries by next morning he would fire a second round perhaps blended with foreign elements, and might fortify himself against counterattack. I did not give him the time for that. I fired a combined volley of reinforced shots at him. They hit the target. There was no struggle. There was no yell. Ngii died like a fowl. His first wife discovered him dead in the morning. Dead, like a stone.

101

His corpse was as black as charcoal because the pellets penetrated his body and did maximum damage to his organs. I had blended our conventional *ngalemudumbu* with a foreign element – thunder. Perhaps Ngii did not expect that quick and devastating retaliatory response to his attack. After all, he had attacked and killed people with impunity. As such he might have taken me for one of the husks and might not have protected himself. Within a few hours his body was covered with blotches as if he had been shot with a million glowing pellets some of which penetrated deep into his body and others that simply lodged below the skin. Before long, the corpse was putrefying and had to be buried quickly. He was buried in a crude coffin without ceremony, without honour, without land, livestock, women and bars. Epoge died. He died like any other person – alone.

After his burial, I sent word to our people in the Diaspora to return. Only a few have harkened. The majority are still out. Some have decided never to return. Others don't even know they belong to Etambeng. Some fear the children of Ngii will attack them if they returned and asked for their parents' lands Ngii had seized. But where is the Ngii? Where are his children?

I know Ngii trained his wives and children in the art of shooting *ngalemudumbu*. Shortly after his death, they tried to eliminate me. I warned them. They continued. I warned them again. But then, a butterfly can settle on the dropping of a tiger but it can never be a tiger. One day, I got red and taught them a bitter lesson. This is his wife *Nyango* Mesang, she can bear witness. I rained hot magma on them. All who attempted were killed. I killed six of them, four boys and two girls before the others fled including *Nyango* Mesang here present. That is why there is nobody in their compound.

If they have the guts to return and any of them tries to disturb the peace, they will get the bitter side of their intransigence. So; that was how Etambeng was. I promise to protect any person who returns to Etambeng. And let me say it without mincing words, all returnees should settle on their land. If any member of Ngii's family tries to disturb the peace, I shall show him/her that there is a difference between he who owns and he who begs.

The Witness
Immediately *Sango* Nkwel'Ngole fished talking, Ngwane got up and addressed the people.

Ngwane
People of Etambeng, you have all listened to *Sen* Nkwel'Ngole. He has told all of you what caused the mass exodus from Etambeng to other villages. He has been ably assisted by the witness and his son Ebune. In spite of his age, he has recounted all. I wonder whether there is any young person here who would have done better. Now, I want all of you to listen. I shall now ask my collaborators to each narrate what prompted them to participate in the execution of the corpse of *Sango* Epoge whom you called at one time in history Ngii, and at another, the Saviour. I want you to listen attentively. I shall not tolerate any questions, drowsiness or any other form of distraction. I am saying this because I want you to get the gist of the stories. And from the gist each and every one of us will do self-examination to see how we contributed to the demise that now plagues Etambeng. I therefore call on my friend Ntongwe to start. *Mue* Ntongwe, come forth. Come forth, let Etambeng hear you.

Chapter Twelve

Ntongwe

People of Etambeng, my name is Ntongwe. It means 'staff of peace'. We all know the significance of the staff of peace. Once a staff of peace is raised where there is a row, calm is restored immediately. I had been a staff of peace until I discovered the truth about myself in the village that I once considered my village – a village I once saw my father labour for diligently in clearing the roads, building bridges and protecting boundaries from other village encroachments, a village that is now a thorn in my flesh, a symbol of my humiliation. It is painful to recall the dehumanizing acts of spiting us, deriding and discriminating against us and preventing us from exercising our God-given economic might simply because, as the people of the village claim, we are alien, we don't belong to them.

I discovered this early in life. Whenever the village went out to clear roads, my father and the people he frequently communed with were given the most difficult portions of the road to clear – portions with stones and spiky grass. When it came to sharing 'state' animals like buffalos, hogs, antelopes, elephants, cows and pigs, my father and his group were never invited to witness the butchering. Whatever dog-meat was sent to them, they took it in good faith. But when it came to going to search for a missing hunter or trapper, they were made to lead the search teams. I remember how in one occasion, a missing hunter was discovered dead and rotten. While the chief and his people avoided the stench, my father and his friends were made to bury the remains. My father and his people never had compounds of their own. Their sheds were always attached to the houses of people whose relationship with them I could not determine as a child.

One day, I saw a beautiful girl and I talked to her about marriage.

"You want me to lose my personality by marrying a refugee? You are refugees here. You can never own farms here. You can never own houses here because your people migrated from Etambeng. If I marry you will you take me to Etambeng? I can't go to Etambeng. I hear the people are terrible wizards. Witchcraft drove your people from there and they dispersed to all neighbouring villages. That is why you are here. At first your people worked for us without pay but now, because they are very good people they work on 'two-party'. Shall we survive on that?" the girl asked.

The world whirled with me. Droplets of sweat sprouted all over my body. I knew at once why my father and his group were treated as outcasts. I allowed the girl go. Then I started investigating what happened that my father and others abandoned their village Etambeng and came to work for people as far as Ngob. Somebody sent me to *Sango* Nkwel'Ngole whom he said was the encyclopaedia of the history of Etambeng. I went and saw him. It was a Saturday – Black Saturday. He told me that my father was the family head of the House of e, e, e, e . That he was a very wise man. Because he was opposed to the late Ngii's barbarism against the people of Etambeng, Ngii, shot him with *ngalemudumbu*). My father became very ill and was taken to Ngob for native treatment. When he recovered, he decided to settle in Ngob. Very soon other Etambeng people, who feared they would be shot by chief Ngii, migrated and met him at Ngob and they formed the outcast group. That is why we are there to be derided by people of a remote village, a village far from the main road, people who under normal circumstances can't measure up to us.

My father died and was buried in a strange land where nobody mentions his name during libation. I expect to exhume his remains and bring them here, and bury them here, and return here, where I belong. But I would not have been dreaming of doing that if the remains of the person who thought he owned Etambeng were still resting in peace in the grave in this village. I had to make them give way to those of my father for them to be given a befitting re-burial in this village – the village of his birth.

Ngwane
Thank you very much. Next person, Etane.

Etane
People of Etambeng, my name is Etane. Etane means light in complexion. And as you see, I am light in complexion. People say I am beautiful. I believe I am. I tend to mesmerize them and they manifest that in various ways – in the number of hand-shakes and hugging greetings they try to force on me each day, the way they stub their feet when they behold me, the way they stammer and blink when they talk to me, and the way their eyes trail me as I pass by.

My mother and I lived at Kako village. One day, one Kako boy proposed marriage to me. I told my mother. She was very delighted hoping perhaps that, that would elevate her status in the village. A few months later, I told my fiancé that I was pregnant. He became very happy and took me to his parents to hasten up the marriage. Although they did not show overt hostility, something told me they weren't happy. I told my fiancé that I sensed that his parents weren't enthusiastic about our engagement. He excused himself by saying that he thought their reaction was the natural way people responded to strange but pleasing situations. I took him for his word. Then my mother fell sick and I accompanied her to a native doctor at Puola. We were there for two months. By the time we returned, my fiancé had been forced to marry another girl. I felt like taking my life. The girl was not more beautiful than I. I saw nothing that made her the preference. I bugged my head for a long time and finally discovered why his parents preferred her to me. She was a daughter of the soil, I was a refugee. I asked my mother where we came from and she told me we came from Etambeng.

When I gave birth, my mother couldn't find a place to bury the afterbirth. Can you imagine that even the boy's father could not show her where to bury the afterbirth? In spite of her painful knees, she trekked four kilometres to bury it on the Etambeng side of the border between Kako and Etambeng where she had buried my father. When she returned I asked her why the people of Kalo could not allow her bury the afterbirth on their soil. Afterbirth is not a corpse. It does not require a lot of land and where it is buried is not marked. She replied that where afterbirth is buried is marked with a plantain. They plant a plantain on the spot. When the plantain bears, it is felled and distributed to the whole village. The villagers eat it as a sign that they have accepted the individual as a member of their village. With that, the individual acquires all the rights and prerogatives of the village – the right to own farmland, marry the girls and vice versa, own building plots, be initiated into village cults and so on and so forth. Most villages refuse granting such indirect citizenship to strangers.

"Now that you have buried my son's placenta on land that is not inhabited, does that mean he belongs to no village?" I asked.

"He belongs to Etambeng. Although birds and monkeys will eat the plantain I have planted on the spot, your son will swear by the placenta that he is an Etambeng child."

"Why had you to bury my father in the bush? Couldn't you carry the corpse to Etambeng?"

"Your father had a very serious dispute with the late chief Ngii. The chief shot him with *ngalemudumbu* and he fell very seriously ill. I carried him and brought him here. *Sango* Meduke, the traditional doctor treated him. When he got well, he went to Etambeng to claim his land the chief had seized. The chief shot him again and I rushed back here with him. We were here for only two days. He died. I sent word to the people of Etambeng to come for the corpse but under the instructions of the chief, none came. I was then forced to plead with these people to carry the corpse to the Etambeng side of the border between the two villages. So I buried him there with the hope that if one day you got married or begot a male child out of wedlock, you would want to exhume the bones of your father and bury them in their rightful place among the ancestors of Etambeng."

People of Etambeng, as you all know, I have a male child out of wedlock and he shall have to exhume the corpse of my father and bury it at Etambeng on the land the late Ngii had seized. To do that, I had to prepare the way by exhuming and destroying the corpse of the Ngii who thought he owned the world.

Ngwane
Very good. Thank you. Next person, Mukala

Mukala
People of Etambeng, I feel extremely bad whenever I think of what happened to me and my brothers and sisters. The worst patient one can handle is the one that defecates where he or she lies. It is horrible. When my father was shot with *ngalemudumbu*, he was decaying alive. Pieces of meat dropped from his putrefying body. Where he lay was where he ate and defecated. He refused to go out of the village for traditional treatment. For several months, my mother took care of him. Then she too fell sick and we the children

109

unaccustomed to taking care of patients took over. My elder sister was the main caretaker. She would call me to support my father at the back for her to bathe him. She would touch every part of my father to wash the sores.

One day, she told me that our father had not defecated for six days because he had not eaten for several days. She said she thought he had constipation. So, she opted to give him enema. When our mother heard that her daughter was about to administer enema to her father, she struggled out of her sick bed and tried to help her. She was almost getting through when she collapsed. We abandoned our father with a belly full of water and went to rescue our mother. As we administered first aid to her, we heard *twaaa*. Our father's anus burst spewing kennel-like droppings all over the place. It required courage and time to sweep the stinking goat-like droppings.

By the time our father died he was all sore. Our father was buried immediately he died. There was no need washing the corpse. There was no need putting it in a coffin. There was no need crying. We thanked God we were relieved of a great burden. But we lost a father. We lost a father who had lost all the love and admiration he deserved. We lost a father who had become an object to be discarded with. And when death supervened, we threw away the object and were relieved for throwing it away. Our father became a thing. He became it. And whenever I cast back my mind at the ordeal we went through, the urge for revenge takes the better of me. My blood becomes gall and I opt for dynamite. That is what propelled me into what I did and how I did it. I have no regrets. I have no fears.

Ngwane
Thank you very much. Next person, Atume.

Atume

People of Etambeng, my name is Atume. Atume means, roast or burn. But when Atume can't burn, and is instead burnt, then there is something very seriously wrong. My story is long but I shall cut it short. I grew up in a village called Iglan. I thought it was my village. We were four who grew up in the same house – one girl three boys.

As I grew up, I noticed that my mother spoke the language of Iglan hesitantly with a heavy accent and that she could not sustain a long conversation in it. She had another language which she spoke to me though I could hardly understand what she said. It surprised me why she spoke the language only to me. It may be she preferred me to speak the language more fluently than that of Iglan. She grumbled in her strange language if something unpleasant happened to her, and sang praise songs in it if something pleasant happened to her. She was hardly enthusiastic about Iglan things. If we won a wrestling match with another village, she would remain detached from the manifestations of joy. I took that as a defect caused by old age.

One day, the village crier announced that it was time to initiate boys who had attained the age of initiation into the various cults – *muankum, ahon, mal, mmpal*. Parents thus started preparing their children for the tests. The cult of *mmpal* (hunting) required that the aspirants recite the names of all 'state' domestic and 'state' wild animals and know where the animals were found in the tribe. The aspirants were expected to know the cries of the animals and be able to distinguish totemic animals from ordinary ones. Every evening, the man I had taken for my father made us recite the names. He drilled us on a number of issues. On the last day of the drill, I thrilled everybody because, though younger, I excelled Nkwete and Nfor. I named in one breath, domestic state animals – cow, horse, hog, ram; and state wild animals elephant, buffalo, lion, tiger, hog, antelope, gorilla and buffoon.

The next day, the three of us went to the forest to inspect our traps. As usual, I caught more animals than the two of them. I caught two porcupines, one hare and two cutting-grass. Nkwete caught a hare and Nfor caught an iguana. Enraged, they started destroying my traps and asking me to return to Etambeng. They said I was exterminating their animals. When I protested, they beat the hell out of me. By the grace of God, I outran them to save my life. I got to the village and reported the incident to our father. He had always appreciated my prowess. Because of the clever traps I set, he was able to run his family without strain. Now, his major help was attacked by non-consequential children. He grew mad and dashed to the forest and got the two fellows well beaten. In beating them he asked whether I was responsible for their ineptness. Wherefore, their mother attacked my mother and asked her to return with her genus to Etambeng. Enraged by what she might have considered bad judgment and lack of appreciation for what I did for the family, and perhaps venting out years of grudges against her, my mother poured insults on her and told her she was ready to return to her hell with her genus and allow her remain in her heaven with her blockheads. After saying that, she started crying in her strange language. Then she told me that though I spoke the language of the people of Iglan with native flair, I did not belong to the village. I was a foreigner. I was a refugee in a village I had thought was my village.

I asked her where Etambeng was found. With swollen eyes, she told me my story – my sad story. She said when I was only a few years old; my father was shot with *ngalemudumbu* in his village Etambeng. She carried him to Iglan for treatment. After a long time, he got well and returned to Etambeng. Within a short time, he was shot again. She was forced to return with him and me to Iglan where he suffered for a long time and died. She said I had spent most of my life on earth in Iglan.

She said that though Nkwete and Nfor had become hostile they had been very wonderful and cordial. She said I should forgive them but never go trapping again because it was out of envying my trapping skills that they became violent. So I stopped going to trap. And as I stopped providing meat for the family, I lost the favour of the man I had taken for my father.

Under those conditions, I thought remaining in Iglan would mean that I shall never get initiated into any cult, never marry and never own property. My mother is old and I have to bring her here, to be buried here. I could not dream of doing so if the remains of Ngii were still found anywhere in Etambeng. They had to be disposed of before I went to exhume my father's corpse and bring the bones here. That is why I meted justice on the corpse of the person in whose hands my father had suffered so much injustice.

Ngwane
Thank you very much. Good. Next person, Dione.

Dione
People of Etambeng, my name Dione means market. And that is what the people who gave us refuge thought of me. They thought I could go out with anybody at anytime. That is, sell myself for money. But that was their wrong interpretation of the name Dione. I interpret my name as, 'worthy of public display, admiration and acquisition'. In other words, I am worthy of public manifestations and consequently chosen for marriage. But can you imagine that in the village where my mother and I grieved over my father's grave, no boy wanted to marry me? Every word of love ended on when I would sleep with a given boy. One day, one boy said he loved me more than the sun that gave the world light. I asked him what aspect of me pleased him so much. He said the totality of me. I told him I loved him

113

also. The next day he brought bundles of gifts. I told him that the bundles of gifts were a sign of bad faith because gifts have the negative force of enticing and persuading. I said the type of love he said he had for me did not require twists and backstabbing manoeuvres like the giving of disproportionate gifts. I advised him to take back the gifts and keep them until he uttered the golden word of love. He asked what that word was and I said if he did not know the golden word of love then of course, he did not love me more than the sun that gave the world light. When he insisted that I tell him, I snapped, "You liar, who do you think you want to deceive, me? Poor you, go your way". The fellow was not the only one who came telling me lies. They didn't want to marry me because I did not belong to their village. But they wanted to sleep with me as a ransom for breathing the air of their village. When they found out that they could not put down the back of my head, they gave me names. They said I was a harlot, a witch and all what not. They turned the women of the village against me.

One day, a certain woman accused me of having slept with her husband. I kept quiet. They took that for acceptance of guilt and continued making noise. My mother asked me and I told her the accusation was false. She too brushed it aside. Then in the evening, the chief and his counsellors came and said I was caught with the husband of Nzike. In anger I told the chief and his people that there was nobody in the whole village capable of entering between my legs. Not a single soul. The chief and the counsellors took offence and said I had under-rated the men of the village and I must leave their village. My mother and I did not take them serious until midnight when they incarnated *Muankum* to chase us out of the village. Can you imagine what it means for refugee women to brave the night in a strange land? *Muankum* escorted us to the border with another village. We trekked to the village and passed the rest of the night by the veranda of a widow. In the morning we told her our ordeal. She opened her doors for us but before we could loosen our cargo and establish ourselves in her house, the chief of Elambet sent emissaries to his counterpart of our new village asking him to chase us out because we were witches. The chief ordered the widow to drive us. So we set going again. At present my mother and I are without a place to put our heads. We are perching in a neighbouring village. So, I want to bring her here for us to resettle here, and later on go to Elambet to exhume the remains of my father and come and bury them here. But I can't do that without marrying. Only men have the prerogatives of exhuming bones. So, I can't exhume the bones of my father unless I am married and my husband spearheads the exhuming. I can't marry if I am not amongst my people. So I have decided to come back home. But I can't come back home to bring the bones of my father and have them share the village with the bones of a person who thought he owned this land.

Ngwane
Thank you. Next person, *Mue* Etone

Etone
People of Etambeng, my ordeal lies in the fact that by the time my father died, he had lost all human dignity. When he was shot with *ngalemudumbu*, he developed a complex disease which most people thought was smallpox. Our family was forced to build him a hut far in the forest where curious children wouldn't have access. He lived there alone. I wonder whether he bathed at all. Only my mother went to the forest to give him food. According to what she told us, they avoided contact with each other in order to prevent contamination and spreading of the disease. Although my father was dying, he was still conscious of protecting his family.

My mother usually carried his food tied in a leaf. She would go to the forest, place the food on a stone in an assigned place and shriek his pseudonym to announce to him that the food was brought. In the early days he would respond with an enthusiastic and re-assuring shriek also. They both used shrieked-pseudonyms to protect each other from evil spirits. It was believed that if a person's real name was used in the forest the person would be possessed by evil spirits. Thus, though my father was firmly in the grip of death, he and my mother were still very protective of each other. They thought they could delude death by giving death-agents wrong signals about each other. Can you imagine what that mystery called marriage can do to devoted couples!

But as the disease got the better of him, his shrieks lost vitality and charm. He could no longer have the human touch even in shriek language. His shrieks grew weaker and weaker till there were no shrieks anymore. At that time the only way my mother ascertained that he was still alive was that she found the food taken away. In spite of no responses, she kept on shrieking to announce that the food was delivered. One day, she discovered that the food was not taken. The next day, the food was not taken. When she returned she told my elder brother. He in turn reported the matter to the head of the *Muankum* cult. *Muankum* took prompt action and searched the forest. It discovered the remains of my father apparently dragged from the hut, half eaten by a wild beast.

The problem now is what killed my father – the wild beast or the disease? That puzzle haunts our family. It is sad to think of it. I mean, it is so unutterably poignant, so heart-rending, so savagely humiliating that I choke and hiccough whenever I find myself asking the question.

I wonder whether with that, I can ever forgive the person who made my father lose human dignity and become food for a wild animal. My father did not lose human dignity alone. We, his family members, lost it with him. He did not die alone. We died with him. We, especially my mother died with him because the thought of what might have happened to him constantly and savagely stabs us. To be candid, whenever I try to picture out how my father might have died, my bowels convulse with the glowing urge for revenge. Not revenge against innocent people but revenge against the culprit no matter his state.

Ngwane
That's good. Thank you. Next person, *Mue* Ngwese.

Ngwese
People of Etambeng, I don't know the meaning of my name Ngwese. It however rhymes with *nwensen* perseverance. If I say it is perseverance then I should say it fits our ordeal. When my father was shot with *ngalemudumbu* and he died and was buried by the roadside on the way to the traditional doctor's place, my mother proceeded with me to a village called Nchumbeng. I grew up in the village with very intimate childhood friends. The man who had given my mother asylum treated us very kindly. I knew it was not my village but there was nothing that made me unhappy with the village until my ignorance plunged me into a serious problem.

Since I did not grow up in the guidance of a father, there were very sensitive traditional issues I did not know about. When I was 14 years old, one man called Ngene, a hunter, got missing in the forest. His immediate family members had gone for a death celebration in a distant village leaving only very little children and an old mama in the compound. So the chief sent for them while the village feigned a frantic search for the missing hunter. For two days village people searched for him.

On the third day, we the young joined in the search. We did not search for long when I screamed that I had found the corpse. That was an abomination. People had been seeing the corpse but had been waiting for the man's immediate family members to return and be led to discovering the corpse. It was imperative that only an immediate family member of the deceased discovered and informed the population that the corpse was found. That was to keep the misfortunes and obligations associated with *eben* (violent death) within the concerned family. Now, there I was. I had ignorantly broken a taboo and by so doing contaminated my family with the misfortunes and obligations associated with violent deaths. What I had thought would bring me honour and praise instead brought me a curse. I needed ritual cleansing. Traditional doctors and House-heads of Nchumbeng had to cleanse me.

My mother cried for four days non-stop because of what the cleansing entailed. She had to buy a cow, seven goats, seven fowls; seven crates of beer, seven bottles of whisky and a number of seven, seven other things. Because everybody knew about her plight, they gave her some time to look for the things. We thus became beasts of burden. We traded in palm oil and any other commodity that would fetch money fast. I remember vividly how we plodded over the hills to sell our commodities in distant markets. By the time we got the money for the ritual items, my mother was a living corpse. We finally, provided them and I was cleansed.

My mother's health soon broke down and deteriorated fast because of the strain. Can you imagine the hell I went through taking care of her? Where she lay was where she defecated. To make sure that she was not nauseating to visitors, since it is customary for people to show good faith by visiting the sick, I unmasked the sonness in me, and wore the mask of a daughter. I cleaned her, bathed her, and did what only daughters are better placed to do to their mothers under such conditions. By the time she died, I was the talk of the day. I had thought the community would be horrified by my dare the devil act of washing her and shun me, but everybody especially the women hailed me for keeping my mother constantly clean. The people of Nchumbeng held me in very high esteem. They helped me give her a befitting burial in a shallow grave. It is four years since. In future, I shall want to exhume her bones and bring them here for final burial. But I would not have been planning to bring her bones here if the bones of Ngii were still lying in peace anywhere in this village. I don't see how I would have allowed the bones of Ngii and those of my mother to share this village.

Ngwane
Fine, thank you very much. Next person, myself.

People of Etambeng, I need not tell you my name. It has been a sing song in this village ever since this matter started. My name has become a household name in this village because of what has brought us here. Very many people believe that I was the mastermind of the event. They are not wrong.

I think I was only seven years old when the calamity that put my life in shambles occurred. Etambeng was in the grip of a terrible pestilence caused by indiscriminate use of *Ngalemudumbu*. People fled in their numbers. One night, a mysterious fog hung all over the village making breathing difficult. As we coughed and gasped for air, our father as if to say enough is enough woke us up and said we should get ready to get out of the village. Where were we going to? People who had migrated to Etaku were said to be moving out because of bad conditions. Those in other villages were not better off. So where were we heading to? None of us knew. Since the order was given we prepared and very soon we were plodding over the hills. We took the road to

Kumenda town. Although the night was chilly and the road rough our father's incessant urges to move on, made us put more spirit into the trekking and to his delight, we arrived the Piananga River Crossing at dawn.

We met thousands of people at the crossing, some queuing up waiting to be crossed, and others sitting dejectedly on stones and beams feeding mosquitoes and midges with their blood. My father felt bad. He had thought being that early at the crossing we would be the first to be crossed. Unfortunately, the thousands of people we met there were also fleeing from the turbulence of their villages. Some said they had spent two days waiting to be crossed. The ferry was pretty old and slow. Although the boys who ran it were marvellous, fatigue and constantly abused by the disgruntled people inflamed and made them hostile even to people who sympathised with them. By 4 o'clock in the evening, my father had not succeeded in bribing his way through. Hunger and insect bites increased a hundred folds towards evening, making the waiting more disgusting. At 6 o'clock, in spite of numerous appeals for one more crossing, the boys stopped work and returned to their base.

Two clandestine canoe boys then came with a raft and at exorbitant prices started ferrying people across the river. By 11 o'clock in the night, they had made five hitch-free crossings – incredibly faster than the official ferry. People beamed with delight and hope, and rushed to pay their fare. Around past midnight, my father secured places for us – my mother, my two elder sisters and three elder brothers. The raft made two other crossings before it came for us. Ours was to be the last crossing for the night and so the raft was made to carry more than twice its capacity. It was so overloaded that it got stuck in the sand and the boys had to work hard to disentangle it. Presently, it set afloat with us, taking a laborious upstream climb along the right bank of the river and after covering about 800 metres, the boys righted its course with a left turn towards the middle of the river. Once we got to the middle, they made the downward turn and allowed the raft to drift on its own downstream with very light manoeuvring aimed at gradually navigating toward the landing on the other side of the river.

We had just begun enjoying the smooth ride when we felt some violent rumbling and trembling underfoot. Our hearts leapt into our mouths as we feared it was either a crocodile attack or the raft was disintegrating. The rumbling was soon followed by abhorrent rocking. The raft tended to gather abnormal speed as it got close to where it would have been navigated toward the landing beacon. The lead boy pinned his navigational pole in the river and pulled hard to slow down the craft and direct it towards the landing. The pole snapped; the raft reeled off course, and dashed past the landing beacon. And there we were, in the middle of the river drifting uncontrollably downstream. After many futile attempts to put the craft on course, the two boys jumped ship leaving us to our fate. Other passengers followed. Only my family and two other passengers remained in the raft. The water seemed to be surging more and more, generating vicious waves which bashed and rocked and tossed the raft up and down.

We clung to the raft praying to be washed to the bank in the dim light of dawn. As we drifted, the lord of the sky was routinely re-instating his authority, dispelling the darkness of the night and instilling hope in the weary and the helpless. The chirps, hoots and croaks of ill-omen agents of night were giving way to the reassuring crows and coos of the fortune-omen agents of day. My father beamed with delight as he saw the approaching break of day upon the monster. He showed incredible courage. He discouraged those remaining on board from jumping into the angry river. He said it was unusual for rivers to flood in November and so thought that our able French-trained engineers might have opened the hatches of one or more hydroelectric dams upstream causing the surging flood that was washing us downstream. He predicted it would soon subside and we'll be able to navigate the raft to the bank of the river. He was very optimistic.

Just as he was speaking, a murderous torrent smashed the raft against the branches of a huge tree which had fallen and planted its branches in the river-bed. The raft disintegrated hurling my brothers and sisters and the other passenger into the furious torrent. They were swallowed up immediately. Only one of them made a desperate cry for help. And that was it.

My father managed to grasp one of the branches above water with his right hand and firmly held me and dragged me from the water with the left. I clung to him in the manner of a small monkey clinging onto its mother. The other passenger had miraculously been thrown onto a big branch and had clung to it. He seized me from my father and made me sit astride and hold firmly to the branch. Then he crawled like a lizard toward my father to assist him save my mother whose legs were caught in a tangle of submerged lianas and branches. It was a horrifying scene.

As the torrent rocked and tossed the branches up and down, left and right, they crushed my mother's legs breaking them at several places and entangling them the more in the lianas and branches. Her agonizing wails and yells stabbed my heart. It was pathetic. The more she made frantic attempts to disentangle herself the more she worsened the situation. As minutes passed by, the yells sank and sank into her throat – degenerating into prolonged agonizing groans that indicated that she was giving up. Now completely disabled and exhausted she could no longer lift up her hands for my father's reach. He on his part had made several fruitless attempts to get to her. Unfortunately because the branch to which he clung was not flexible enough to droop and so lower him within reach of her, he abandoned it for a more flexible smaller one. It drooped sufficiently with him and gave him access to her. He grasped her and tried to yank her out of the tangle. She yelled heartbreakingly. She yelled again and again, her voice gradually sinking. Each dying yell told its pathetic story and bruised my heart with the savagery of a dagger. Then she sounded the last post. My hair stood on end. My father instinctively lowered her to ease her up. But as if to say pity was not the best solution to the debacle, he yanked her again more forcefully and lifted her towards us. The other passenger stretched his right hand to grip her and lift her onto our branch. He fell short of reaching her and while he tried to adjust his position, the small branch on which my father was clinging and holding my mother in the manner a cat carries its young, unable to bear their weight, snapped and plunged them into the wild raging torrent. At that time, the torrent was more than doubled. We watched with horror as the monster pitilessly swallowed up my parents. And that was it. Within a split second, I lost every member of my family.

We remained on the branch till around 10 o'clock in the morning when a search team came and picked us up. The river had miraculously subsided to normality, easing the work of the rescuers. While in their craft, they told us that apart from the two ferry boys, all those who jumped into the river perished and their bodies were littering the banks of the river like dead fish in river-poisoning fishing.

I was then taken to Etaku rehabilitation centre for the homeless. Only Etaku had such facilities. And there, I grew up. I was, so to speak, well treated by the people. Judged from the public face, I would say the people of Etaku loved me. They called me an exceptionally blessed boy – the icon of God's love and mercy. They displayed me in churches and charity organizations and collected alms and donations on my behalf. So long as they were concerned, I was different from all other rascals from Etambeng. With that, my little heart loved them too. Yet in the sphere of love, there is a void in me. There is a void in me because there is no love that can replace family love. And being dispossessed of family love on that black November day, the day God blinked, I call on the international community to strike off that day, month and year from the calendar of human history. Not only should the month of November not have a sixth day, there should neither be a month called November, nor a year known as 1982 in the history of mankind.

Yes, before we acted the way we acted, whenever I thought of that devastating experience I focused every iota of hate toward the epicentre of my undoing. I invited all aggrieved sons and daughters of Etambeng to meetings and planned how best we would punish the person who was responsible for our plight. Today, thanks to the exploits of *Sango* Nkwel'Ngole, I can say with some degree of satisfaction that I did what I was forced to do. It may be contrary to the ethics of civilization but I have no regrets.

Yes, good, thank myself. Next person, *mue* Mekoge.

Mekoge

My name is Mekoge, the son of late chief Mukete of this Etambeng village. I am his last son. I was not a child when all hell broke out at Etambeng and people were fleeing in their hundreds. People fled from their village of birth to become refugees in backward villages where they were humiliated and derided. In fact, what happened is hair-raising and downright unacceptable. Mothers fled leaving their children behind. People carried whatever little thing they could carry to sustain them for a few days in exile.

My father had earlier been carried to Kodmin village for treatment. It was alleged the new chief Ngii, had shot him with *ngalemudumbu* in order to eliminate him and silence his claim to the throne. Because it was evident that he targeted all of us, the offspring of my father, we all took off to different directions, to the unknown. Those who had long breath and strong legs went far. Those with short breath remained within range of his *ngalemudumbu*. I happened to be one of those with long breath and strong legs. I had no choice. I had been named heir apparent, and therefore a primary target. So, I went far, very far, so far that I found myself alone. Because of the distance, I was cut off from news. I shan't dwell on my ordeal in the mountains. It was a sad experience, very sad.

One day, I dreamt my father died. I developed dry throat and instant palpitation. I knew my mother had once again taken my father to the traditional doctor at Kodmin before we fled the village. My father's illness might have aggravated and he might have died. With a village in complete disarray, will there be anybody to organize his funeral? Where will they bury him? The usurper chief was claiming all land. I thought things over. Fear struck me hard. I told my host I would dare a return to my village or visit my parents at Kodmin the next day.

"Do you say your father was taken to Kodmin?"

"Yes. My mother took him there."

"Then why not take this shortcut to Kodmin and go and visit them? From here to Kodmin is only four hours. The road is easy to follow. You can easily distinguish between a bush path and the main road even in the plain forest. Go to Kodmin instead of returning to Etambeng by the way you came here. By the way you came here will take you about two days of very hard trekking to get there."

The next day, I left Elaamin village for Kodmin. The road was easy to follow. By mid afternoon, I saw signs of a village. There were dispersed farms on nearby hills. The vegetation had moved from thick forest to savannah. I descended a hillock and in the valley I met some children fetching water. I asked them where they came from. They said they came from Kodmin. I helped them carry their water containers and made them lead the way to the village. As we moved on, I asked them whether there was any problem in the village. They said there was no problem. We soon got to the main road. I asked where the road we were leaving on the right went to. They said it went to Etambeng. Just a few metres from the spot where I asked the last question, was a mound that looked like a fresh grave. Dreams have a surrealistic influence over me. I recalled the dream I had about my father's death, the dream that made me undertake to visit them and my hair stood on end when I saw the mound. A mystical force drew me to it. A million deep and snaky cracks crisscrossed the mound and large headed soldier ants shuttled in and out of the cracks yanking large pieces of who-knows-what in and out of the mound. An eerie sensation made me lose my bearings. Tears flooded into my eyes. I wiped them and tried to catch up with the children.

"Do you say nothing serious has happened in the village?" I asked.

"Nothing," they responded.

I wiped my eyes and blamed myself inwardly for being chickenhearted and emotional. If my father, a deposed chief had died, the children would have known. He was a well known chief before his demise at Etambeng. And if he had died, there would have been a large crowd that would have made the children and every other person know that an important personality had died. When we reached the village I asked one of the children to take me to the chief's compound. I knew the chief would know where my father was receiving treatment. At the chief's compound, I bumped into my mother. She was in mourning regalia. She fixed a million watt gaze at me, and I, at her. An inexplicable force held us breathless for some time. Then, as if loose from a stranglehold, she leapt into the air and crashed onto the ground crying. I instinctively yelled and as we cried and the neighbourhood heard a masculine cry interlace a feminine cry, people rushed from all over the place to see the people they had been waiting for – the people from Etambeng.

1st Man

I think that is the late man's child. He's a carbon copy. Perhaps the people of Etambeng have sent him ahead to come and tell us that they were coming to carry the corpse of their deposed chief.

2nd Man

Is that the way we do it? Is it he who owns the head who shaves it? In other words, is it the bereaved themselves who run errands? If what you are saying were true, he would not have travelled alone. Those people of Etambeng are mad. We have sent several emissaries to tell them about the death of their deposed chief and their obligation to come and carry the corpse to their village and give the chief a befitting burial. But they tend not to care.

3rd Man

Poor chief, we horridly buried him when sympathizers could bear the stench no more. The corpse was already at an advanced stage of decay and that forced us to bury it in a shallow grave to ease exhumation. We had waited for three days. So even if they came now, they will have to wait for two or more years before they exhume the bones and carry them to that their murderous village. Stories we hear about that village are mortifying.

Mekoge

Customarily, a man is not supposed to cry for long. When the chief found that it was taking the women too long to stop me from crying, he came in forcefully and bellowed,

"Who is this crying like a woman! Who do you expect to wipe your tears? When your father talked to me about you, I knew he had a person to avenge his death. Now you cry – betraying the woman in you. Will crying resurrect your father? A man has killed your father. Do you say you are not a man? Or should people now console with you 'mami no cry yaa'?" he asked.

That reproach emboldened me. I wiped my eyes, coughed, drew the mucus into my mouth, moved out of the house and spat it out. Then I told my mother to take me to the grave. She led me to the dreadful mound I had predicted. Tears welled into my eyes. I wiped them several times trying to suppress a choking outburst. My father had died like a fowl, had been buried like a dog and so, the village children did not know that something serious had happened in the village. Can you imagine that? Can I ever forgive the cause of that disgrace?

People of Etambeng, I have not had the opportunity to settle scores conventionally, but I plan to go and exhume my father's corpse from the remote village in which it is buried. Before I do so, the corpse of the person who thought he owned Etambeng had to make way for the triumphant entry of my father's corpse. And that is it. There is no regret for what I have done.

Ngwane
Thank you very much. I shall now call on *mue* Mukala to tell you how we meted justice on the corpse of the tyrant.

Chapter Thirteen

Mukala

People of Etambeng, I am called Mukala. The name means White man. I am a White man. I don't like dirt. I don't eat shit. I don't mince words. I was instrumental in exhuming the corpse of the late chief Ngii. Ngii means lion. He gave himself that name with the intent of dethroning chief Mukete Epalle. Epalle means he-goat — an animal with a mane but no fangs, a grass-eating animal with a mane. After juxtaposing the demise of the flesh-eating animal and the grass-eating animal, and basing our findings on what *Sango* Nkwel'Ngole had told us we decided to act. We exhumed the corpse of Ngii, tried it, found it guilty and hanged it.

It was a daunting operation. We got to the grave at about nine in the evening, not because we were afraid to dig out the corpse in the day time, but because it was more convenient to do so in the night. We knew it would take about half the night to dig the corpse out. Ngwese started the digging. After softening the hard surface soil, Ngwane removed the soil with his shovel. We took turns and very soon, we hit the coffin. When the girls heard Ngwane's pick axe hit it twice, they demanded what made the uncanny sound. "We have got to the coffin," he said in a guffaw. The girls started shivering from fear.

I moved onto them and told them that dead men don't bite. In spite of that Dione firmly clung onto Etane. Ngwane soon jumped out of the grave and signalled Ngwese to take his turn. Ngwese sulked. I jumped into the grave in his place, cleared the coffin of the soil around it and passed three ropes under it and held out their ends at both sides of the grave. Six of my companions took hold of the ends of the ropes and waited for me to jump out. Once out, I ordered them to pull. They pulled hard but the coffin stuck onto the bottom of the grave. I jumped back into the grave and using a lever, shook the coffin several times and jumped out again. My companions pulled hard again and the stubborn coffin was finally lifted to the surface. We all were jubilant. The girls picked up courage. The next thing we had to do was to carry the coffin to the place of trial. We had chosen as trial ground, the crest of mount Ebang overlooking the village. How were we to carry a coffin from which body fluids dripped?

I had expected that and had made a wheel. I brought the wheel and mounted it under the coffin. We tied ropes to the coffin and while some of us pulled, others pushed it until we got to the top of mount Ebang early in the morning. We were so exhausted that we could not congratulate ourselves for that marvellous achievement. We simply slumped onto the soft grass on the mount and slept. By the time we got up it was early afternoon.

Ngwane
People of Etambeng, it is only half past eleven and I see some of you dozing. That is an insult to those who are telling the stories. They are not telling stories for the sake of telling pleasant stories. They are telling stories for you to imbibe them and know what made the elephant trample the crab. Your dozing is tantamount to disregard of the seriousness of the case before you. To stop you from such intransigence I would want all of you to stand. Please all stand. Anybody found sitting will be made to kneel down in the centre. I am not kidding. Please stand while Mukala continues.

The Witness
The frightened people stood. After some time, they were ordered to sit down and, listen.

Mukala

Trial started at three o'clock. I broke the coffin open and overturned it. Chief Ngii rolled out like a deflated ball face down. Ngwese screwed his face in anger and turned the limp thing face up and slapped it square in the face. Its mouth opened as if to ask for pardon.

Ngwese

Why are you hiding your face, you fool? You will have to answer questions. You are charged with crimes against humanity. Since you are mute and humble, we shall ask nature to be your defence counsellor. If we ask you a question needing *yes* or *no*, a puff of the wind would stand for *yes*, and the stillness of the wind would stand for *no*. Do you hear?

Mukala

Ngwese took the silence for *no*, so he repeated the question. There was a puff of the wind and we took that for *yes*. The case thus started.

Ngwese

Chief Ngii, it is alleged you usurped the chieftaincy seat of Etambeng and in a bid to stop any contest for it, you shot its rightful claimant with *ngalemudumbu* and he was struck with *mbim*. He went for treatment at Kodmin and for five years he received treatment and was recovering. But when he visited Etambeng to see his subjects and land, you unleashed the most overwhelming volley of shots at him. He was rushed back to the place of treatment but died soon after. You foiled all attempts to bring his corpse home for a descent burial. Are you guilty or not guilty?

Mukala

Puff of wind says guilty.

Ngwese
It is said that after eliminating the chief you directed your attention on House-heads. You unleashed untold barbarism against them. You indiscriminately shot *ngalemudumbu* at them and their families and they suffered from all sorts of diseases. This caused the majority of Etambeng people to flee to neighbouring villages especially Etaku. Today, three quarters of Etambeng population is out. You wanted to exterminate the old generation in order to create a structure that would know only about you and not the rightful claimants of the throne of Etambeng. Are you guilty or not guilty?

Mukala
A puff of wind says, guilty.

Ngwese
You seized farmland that belonged to House-holdings and gave them to your family members. Your family members, non-original citizens of Etambeng owned three quarters of the fertile land of Ekambeng. You seized people's livestock and sent them to the villages of your maternal and paternal uncles for safe keeping. Are you guilty or not guilty?

Mukala
A puff of wind says, guilty.

Ngwese
Now you are guilty as charged. And because of that you shall be executed by hanging.

Mukala and Others
As it pleases the court.

Mukala

After the judgment which by all human standards was free, fair and humane, I proceeded to perform the execution. We put back the corpse in the coffin, built a high platform with poles loosely put in place but whose stability was assured by firmly tied crossbars at all the four corners. We then carried the coffin and placed it on the platform. I climbed on the platform, raised the head of the corpse, put a hood over it, then put the noose of the hang rope round the neck and climbed down the platform. I then climbed on a tree branch and tied the hang rope on a branch. After that, I climbed down and asked Dione to lead us in prayer.

Dione

Oh Lord God, Creator of Heaven and Earth,
Most merciful and everlasting God,
We your over aggrieved children are here and
Now about to carry out retributive justice on the
Corpse of a person who so offended the world
That the world that he thought he owned and
Could do things with impunity has discarded
Him and thrown him to you his maker.
Father do whatsoever pleases you with him.
Father, we have judged his flesh.

You will judge his soul lord, we are not being
Revengeful but deterrent and so we place
Our mission into your hands. May the fate that
Now befalls Ngii befall his kind the world over.
Amen.

All of Us

Amen.

Mukala

After the prayer, we undid the crossbars that held the platform in place. The four cardinal poles were now loose. I tied a rope to each of them and held the four ropes together and then waited for the execution officer in chief to give the supreme order. He tended to mull over something. He grimaced confusedly, regained stability, raised his right hand and counted, 4, 3, 2, 1, pull. I pulled. The structure collapsed in a loud combined whooshing, clanging, and crashing noise followed by a squelch. The coffin fell on the poles leaving the corpse to dangle on the rope. There was no pain, there was no twisting. There was only the loss of human dignity.

As the body of Ngii remained hanging, gently swayed by the wind that had been the prosecution counsellor, we thought of what next to do. The girls complaining of nausea wanted it buried immediately on the spot. Ngwese, Ntongwe and Ngwane decreed that Ngii's remains were not to have any trace anywhere on earth. They said they had to be cremated and the ash thrown into the River Piananga. Since he would have no grave anywhere, his wives, sons and daughters would have nowhere to lay claim of inheritance. Nobody would remember him during libations. He would vanish as spittle vanishes in a river.

Mekoge

I broke the coffin into pieces, cut the poles into pieces and all of us fetched more wood and made a large pile of dry wood under the hanging corpse. Then Ntongwe climbed on the branch on which the corpse was hanging and cut the rope. The corpse and the rope crashed on the pile of dry wood. Then I stretched out the corpse. In other words, I spread its hands and legs so that they could burn as single entities. Then we fetched wet wood and arranged it first round the corpse, then on it. In fact we sandwiched the corpse between the dry and wet wood. That done, we waited for Atume to bring the things we had sent him to bring from his village of refuge. It was the nearest village to where we were. He brought jute bags, palm oil and drinking water. We poured a lot of palm oil on the pile and set it ablaze. The inferno that followed was incredible.

People as far as Nongomadiba and Echugenyo said they saw the flames high into the sky and thought a village was blaze. The heat drove us from the spot. Mukala advised that we camp below the blaze and if the whole forest caught fire we would have the possibility of escaping. For two nights, the fire burned on the same spot. Not a single blade of grass caught fire elsewhere though tree leaves around withered. For two nights we were encamped watching the effacing of the traces of a tyrant. By the time things cooled down, there was nothing left but the trace of a human form in the ashes. We gathered the ashes, put them in two jute bags and carried them to the Piananga River and emptied the bags into the river. Then we burnt the bags and threw the ash too in the river.

Atume

When we returned from the Piananga River, we went to Ndoh to condole with the mother of a witchcraft victim. It was there that we met *Nyango* Mesang, the widow of late chief Ngii and we told her in her face what we had done to her late husband's corpse and what we shall do to any person who is accused of witchcraft in our midst from now on. We are not kidding. We have formed anti-witchcraft brigades in this village and we are having branches in other villages.

Chapter Fourteen

The Witness

And so it happened that the children everybody thought had committed an abomination and would be shamefaced in telling stories about it, held the people of Etambeng hostage in the grove and told them what they had done and how they had done it. Ngoe and Eseme who had said the children would flee from Etambeng were lip shut. What the people called a grisly crime, the children celebrated as a great achievement.

People call me the fly because they say I bear witness to the most secret events. But throughout my life, I have never witnessed a situation like this. I have never seen children so adamant, so uncouth, so disgusting, yet so admirable.

Etambeng people sat face down, confounded, flabbergasted, stupefied and frightened. Nobody coughed. Nobody tried to sneak away. Even *Sango* Nkwel'Ngole did not stir where he sat. For sure he did not expect the spine-tingling stories. I tried to sneak away but could not under the watchful and stern bloodshot eyes of Ngwane. It was horrible.

After a punishing one hour of grave silence coupled with self-examination and self-reproach, the people of Etambeng were relieved when apparently, *Sango* Nkwel'Ngole remembered that he had been promised maximum protection by the children. He signalled that he wanted to be carried back home. Four of the children promptly got the sofa in which they had brought him to the grove, sat him in it and carried him leaving the rest of the people under the watchful eyes of the remaining three boys and two girls. While *Sango* Nkwel'Ngole was being carried away, Etambeng people relaxed their numbed limps to allow blood flow in them once more. I raised my hand and indicated that I wanted to blow my nose and cough. I was granted permission. I made a few steps from the grove, took a sharp bend and sneaked away leaving the people of Etambeng to handle their demise the way they wanted. I left them to decide what to blame – the lianas that entangled the elephant or the elephant that dragged them and pulled down the forest. Too bad, perhaps too good. *Abuu-* shit.